TIMES LIKE THESE

TIMES LIKE THESE

A NOVEL

E. E. SMITH

PHOENIX INTERNATIONAL, INC.

FAYETTEVILLE

Inquiries should be addressed to:
Phoenix International, Inc.
17762 Summer Rain Road
Fayetteville, Arkansas 72701
Phone (479) 521-2204
www.phoenixbase.com

Library of Congress Cataloging-in-Publication Data

Smith, E. E. (Evelyn Eileen), 1932–
  Times like these : a novel / E. E. Smith.
    p. cm.
  ISBN 978-0-9824295-9-4 (alk. paper)
  I. Title.
  PS3619.M582T56 2011
  813'.6—dc23

                                2011024645

My sister once took a book out of the library because she thought it had an interesting title: *My Parents Were Lulus*. But when she started to read it she discovered that it was written by a doctor in Africa, and the title was actually *My Patients Were Zulus*.

I dedicate this book to the loving memory of my sister Margaret (1925–2006), and know that she would enjoy the joke. You see, *our* parents really *were* lulus.

Contents

Preface

"Times like these are about as unpredictable as boarding-house stew!" says Teddy Soberjowski in the previous book, *Boardinghouse Stew.* The year was 1943, in the early days of World War II, when no one knew for certain what would happen next.

Now, in 1945, the times are no more predictable than they were then. Less so, in fact, for the young heroine of the present book, *Times Like These.*

She was only eleven years old when she convinced Mrs. Mumson, the proprietress of a seedy, down-at-heel boardinghouse in Sacramento, that she was "going on thirteen" in order to get a job as a maid for the summer. Due to a critical manpower shortage in the California capital, Mrs. Mumson had no other candidates for the job, so she was hired. Now she really *is* thirteen and on her way to a new home in Nevada, and an uncertain future with her parents, who have only recently reconciled—again.

Her champion at the boardinghouse, Teddy Soberjowski, is gone but not forgotten (as the writing of *Boardinghouse Stew,* six decades later, would prove).

By June of 1945 the war was over in Europe but not in the Pacific, where it raged on, amid heavy casualties. It had also taken a terrible toll on the health of President Roosevelt, who died in April of that year. Now Harry Truman was president and, unbeknown to all but a few, contemplated using a horrific new weapon to force Japan to surrender, thereby saving American lives.

What would happen next?

Teddy's pronouncement had never been more relevant: *"Times like these are about as unpredictable as boardinghouse stew!"*

TIMES LIKE THESE

CHAPTER ONE

Traveling on a Pass

Wear your little seersucker suit, my mother's last letter advised.
*It won't show the wrinkles so much. You'll be traveling on a pass,
so you won't have a sleeper.*

She didn't need to tell me. We always traveled on passes,
and we never had a sleeper. My father was a telegrapher on
the Western Pacific Railroad, which allowed him and his
family to travel on passes anywhere the railroad went, but
we had to spend our days and nights in the coach. Why
should this trip be any different? And yet, I thought,
smoothing the skirt of my little blue-and-red-plaid seersucker suit, it *was* different. I was traveling alone, without
my mother.

Exactly two years ago, in June of 1943, I had lied about
my age (among other things) to Mrs. Mumson, the owner
of the boardinghouse where I was applying for a job as a
maid for the summer. I needed a job desperately, and I was
willing to do almost anything to get one. Without earning
the money for it, I would never have a bicycle of my own,
so I told Mrs. Mumson that I was *"going"* on thirteen. (I
was really only eleven.) Now, I thought with a rush of
excitement, I actually *was* thirteen! And traveling alone, for
the first time in my life.

The other lie I had told Mrs. Mumson was about my
name. I said it was Eileen, which was only *half* a lie, because
that was my middle name. I hated my first name, which is

Evelyn, so I assumed a new identity along with my new job. But out here there would be no escaping it. My father was sure to call me "Evelina," pronouncing it "Eveleeeena," and punctuating it with a wink and a poke in the ribs. My mother's name was Rosa Frederika, after her two German grandmothers. She didn't like her name, either, so she called herself "Rosalie." My father would sometimes call her "Freddie," but he knew better than to wink and poke *her* in the ribs!

I wondered what they were calling each other out here, in the Great American Desert, as it was labeled on the map I looked the place up on. Observing my parents over the years I had developed a system for knowing if they were getting along—or not. On the rare occasions when things were going well, besides "Freddie" my father might call her "Rosie," and she would call him "Paddy" or just "Pad." When things were not going well, it was a frosty "Mother" and "Daddy." When things were *really* bad, it was *"Rosa!"* and *"George!"*

Not that they saw much of each other. My mother and I lived in Sacramento and my father lived in any number of funny little towns in northern California and Nevada, moving from one place to another with the Western Pacific. "When they get inside *plumbing,*" my mother would say in exasperation, "he wants to *move!*" She seemed to have nothing but contempt for the way he lived, which was all too primitive for her taste. Though George "Paddy" Smith could look quite dapper on his infrequent visits to our house in Sacramento, wearing a fedora and a double-breasted suit, sometimes with a flower in the buttonhole, it

My father, George "Paddy" Smith

was obvious that he preferred another kind of life. He knew every trainman on the railroad and most every hobo, too, in the "jungles" along the track. During the Depression he maintained that there were a lot of fine, intelligent gentlemen out there in the camps, who were "just down on their *luck,* Mother." But her response was always the same. Luck had nothing to do with it. Your fine, intelligent gentlemen had *money,* and they dined at home on a linen tablecloth and bone China—not sitting around a campfire, eating beans out of a can. The very idea!

My father would sigh and say, "You can't tell a German anything, can you Eveleeena?" Then he would wink and poke me in the ribs.

I never did understand why my parents married in the first place, being such complete opposites. Though I had heard often enough that "opposites attract," I knew firsthand that they also *repel.* My mother was very religious, being (at the moment) a Christian Scientist, and my father was an avowed atheist. She was a teetotaler; he drank like a fish. Though she was middle class, at best, she was also a snob; he was the most broad-minded of men. She disapproved of all forms of gambling; he was the world's best poker player. I know of only one picture of my parents *as a couple.* It was taken on their honeymoon, in 1917—a motorcycle trip, camping and fishing along the way—just the sort of thing my mother would hate. *No wonder she looks so unhappy!*

With all their differences my parents quarreled, separated and also divorced, but remarried—at least twice, to my knowledge. Even that day, as I kept track of the passing mileposts between my old home in Sacramento, California

My parents as a couple

(milepost No. 138), to my new home in Shafter, Nevada (No. 766), I wasn't really sure if they were married or divorced! Keeping track of my parents had always been difficult.

"Excuse me, sir," I said politely, leaning across the aisle in the coach and addressing a kindly looking gentleman there. "Could you tell me what time it is, please?"

The gentleman laid aside his newspaper and took out a big gold watch on the end of a chain across his vest. *It was just like Daddy's.* "Why, yes, certainly. Let's see now, it's twenty minutes 'til six." Carefully replacing the watch in his pocket, he peered at me over small reading glasses. *Daddy didn't use reading glasses.* "I expect you're getting hungry, eh, Miss?"

"Oh, no," I replied with a little laugh. "I can wait." *Wait for what? Starvation?*

According to my calculations, 5:40 meant the train was already two hours late. During the war, passenger trains rarely ran on schedule. Among the three classes of trains, they were given the lowest priority by the railroad. Military transport, or troop trains, as they were called, came first, then freight. Passenger trains—even the proud Exposition Flyer, which ran on these very tracks—had to take a siding, sometimes for hours, and wait for the freight and troop trains to pass.

I had never ridden the Exposition Flyer, though I saw it once "flying" through the Sacramento Valley on its way west. It took its name from the Golden Gate International Exposition in San Francisco in 1939, and was inaugurated to carry passengers between the East Coast and San Francisco

A Western Pacific Exposition Flyer. *Courtesy the California State Railroad Museum*

for the fair. But it had proved to be such a popular train that it ran long after the fair closed, and was still running today, six years later.

This train was hardly in a class with "The Flyer," being a so-called "milk run" that delivered passengers, Railway Express (and maybe even milk) to every whistle-stop along the way. Nevertheless, we were all subject to the same rules, being shunted into a siding to let the freights and troop trains go through. There seemed to be a lot of them today, which meant I would arrive at my destination half-starved. To make matters worse, the dining-car steward was coming through the cars announcing the first call to dinner. I tried to avoid the curious eyes of the gentleman across the aisle by taking an intense interest in the scenery (which was anything but interesting).

Hours went by and it was simply more of the same—sand and sagebrush, unrelieved by greenery, except in the scrubby gardens in little towns along the way. Now it was getting dark and the third call for dinner had been announced. I hadn't eaten anything since my small breakfast and I was beginning to feel faint. *If only Mommy had sent me more money!* I supposed she thought I had enough, but I had used the last of my allowance to buy Mrs. Todd a thank-you gift. She was a neighbor in Sacramento who had been nice enough to let me stay with her and finish the seventh grade after my mother left to join my father out here. Mrs. Todd had a husband in the Seabees who was away for months at a time, so she was glad for my company, she said.

"E'scuse me, Miss," said a deep voice. I turned away from the window and looked up—and up, and up!—until I came to a black face above a stiff white cotton jacket and apron. His large head, capped by closely cropped black hair, almost touched the ceiling. I guessed that he was either a dining-car steward or a cook. (The apron was none too clean.)

"Who . . . me?"

"Yassum," said the man. "I b'lieve yo' daddy want you in de dining cah."

"Oh, but . . . he isn't on this . . ." I was craning my neck and looking around to see who he might possibly have confused me with.

"He say 'right away,' Miss . . . Dis yo' bag?" The man was

pulling my little cardboard suitcase off the rack above my head.

"Well . . . yes . . . but—"

"Come on, den." He was waiting for me to step by him into the aisle, so I led the way toward the door at the end of the car, clutching my white straw hat and little plastic purse while the big man carried my suitcase. There was something about him—apart from his remarkable size— that convinced you to do what he told you.

When we reached the vestibule between the cars, I turned and shouted over the wind and noise, "I'm afraid there's been a mistake. My daddy isn't on this train. He's in—"

Grinning broadly, which showed one polished gold tooth in the front, the man said, "Oh, I knows dat, Miss."

What *was* going on?

Other passengers, seeing a white girl being escorted through the cars by a giant black man in an apron, must have been wondering the same thing. When we reached the dining car I spotted a sign on the door: DINING CAR CLOSED. I stopped and looked questioningly at the big man. *Now what?* But he simply reached past me, pushed open the door, and led me to a table next to the galley. All the other tables were empty, but I could see several more black men in white jackets and aprons in the galley. They all smiled at me and looked knowingly at one another. The big man slid my bag under the table and handed me a menu. Instantly, my famished eyes swept over the choices: Pan-fried Mountain Trout, Baked Ham with Country Gravy and Biscuits, Chicken and Dumplings . . . pies, cakes . . . More food than I had seen in a month, but I had to put a stop to this.

I blurted out, "I . . . I don't have any *money!*"

"We figure dat's why you don' come in fo' dinnuh. An' lunch, too." He was glancing over his shoulder and nodding to the rest of the crew, who nodded back. "Still, we cain' let Mistuh Smith's li'l girl go hungry, kin we?"

"You know who I *am?*"

"Why, honey-chile, we *all* knows yo' daddy!" More smiles and nods from the crew in the galley. "He tol' me, 'Rafe,'—dat's my name, but sometime he call me 'Zulu'— cain' half think *why!*" With this he gave a great guffaw and slapped his knee. "Yo' Daddy tol' me, 'Rafe, my li'l girl's gone be on your train come Thursdee an' I be oblige if you an' de boys look aftuh her.' So . . ."

"But how'd you recognize me? You've never seen me before." *And I'd sure remember if I'd ever seen you before!*

"I see you git on in Sacramen'a, and I say, dat's Mistuh Smith's li'l girl right dere, 'cause you look jes like him . . . Only a whole lot purtier!" At that, the men in the galley all laughed out loud and pounded one another on the back.

I could feel my cheeks burning with embarrassment. Well, it was true, what he said—up to a point. I *did* look like my father. My older sister had inherited our mother's dark-brown hair and eyes, but I had our father's sandy hair, green eyes, and freckles. I was tall and thin like him, too. People always said that I was the "image of my father." And maybe that's why my mother and I never got along. She never got along with my father, either.

I have said that my father was a gambler, and the world's

best poker player. I played with him (but never for money, of course). Every trainman up and down the line lost to him, and he held their IOUs, or "markers," if they couldn't pay, but never called in a debt during hard times. There was a kind of barter system between them, however. A favor, a good turn, help in one form or another could reduce what you owed. He seemed to have a big ledger in his head for keeping track of it all. Over a heaping plate of chicken and dumplings I figured it out: *Rafe, and probably every one of those guys in the galley, owe my father money.*

I was working my way through a second piece of apple pie à la mode (for a skinny kid I could eat a lot), when the dining-car door opened and a white man in a shiny black suit with brass buttons walked in. He was carrying a smooth black leather book and a string of paper tickets. I looked up in panic. What was the conductor going to say about *this?*

Taking in the scene—the diner supposedly closed for the night, no one but one ravenous teenager at a table, the cooks and stewards all looking like a bunch of cats who'd just swallowed the canary—the conductor singled out Rafe for his first question. "What's going on in here?"

Rafe said calmly, "Well, Mistuh Sampson, dis here is Mistuh Smith's chile, goin' out to stay wit' her daddy. Seem she done slep' through the dinnuh calls, so we open up fo' her, special."

Mr. Sampson frowned. "Mister Smith . . . ?" Then a smile crinkled the edges of the shrewd brown eyes behind wire-rimmed bifocals. "So, you're Paddy's girl!"

"Yes, sir," I said, laying down my fork as though I had been caught in the act of committing a robbery.

"Well, well! I should have guessed who it was when you showed me your pass, back there in the coach. Didn't connect the name. Lots of Smiths in this world, you know." He gave a short laugh, and indicated that I should go on eating. "Rafe and his boys been treating you all right, have they?"

"Oh, yes sir!"

"Good. Good. It's going to be a long night, I'm afraid. We're hours late already, and I'll wager you won't get much sleep, sitting up in that crowded coach." Then, opening his leather book and thumbing quickly through the flimsy pages, "I think we might find a berth in a Pullman for this young lady, don't you, Rafe?"

"Yassuh, Mistuh Sampson."

"Now, let's see . . . Looks like we've got a couple of empty berths in Car 14. Might give her one of those, eh?"

"Yassuh, Mistuh Sampson. Dat's what I been thinkin'." *And why you brought my suitcase in here, you sly devil!*

"I'll leave you to it, then. See she has a bite of breakfast in the morning, too, Rafe." Then, turning to me, "Tell your dad hello for Jack Sampson, will you?"

"Yes, sir, I will. Thank you."

As he turned and left the dining car, I wondered how much Mr. Sampson owed my father.

After that heavy meal I began to feel very sleepy. Rafe caught me yawning. "Well, I s'pect we bettuh fine you a bed," he said, retrieving my little suitcase from under the table. "Cah Fo'teen up dis-away," and he pointed toward the front of the train. I started to follow him, then made a quick stop at the galley door to thank the rest of the crew for a fine dinner. *I'll tell Daddy about you, too.*

Passengers in the Pullman cars had already retired for the night, with double tiers of black curtains drawn together and buttoned to ensure privacy. Rafe led me halfway down the aisle of Car 14, stopping in front of an empty lower berth. He said he would come back to wake me in the morning, and tossed my bag inside. I crawled in after it, pulled the curtains shut, and fell asleep seconds later, still in my little seersucker suit.

"Wake up, honey-chile. We almos' dere! And we don' hardly *slow down* fo' Shafter!"

I couldn't believe the night had passed so quickly, but there was the sun, streaming though the streaky windows next to my berth. I rubbed my eyes and threw open the black curtains. Rafe was standing in the aisle with a little tray. On it was a mug of hot cocoa and an assortment of fresh pastries. I took the tray, but asked anxiously, "Are we really almost there? Will I have time to eat this?"

"Sho' you will. Be 'bout a ha'f hour—maybe mo' if we gets shunted off t' the side ag'in." Then he said he'd come back later, and left me sitting up in the berth, drinking my cocoa and watching the scenery going by the window. If I had hoped it would improve overnight, I was disappointed.

A little more than a half hour later, I was standing in the vestibule of the Pullman car, wearing my straw hat trimmed with red and blue ribbons, and nervously clutching the little white plastic purse. The train was slowing down. I heard it blowing for a crossing: WOOOO . . . WOOOO . . . Woop . . . WOOOOOOOO. Two longs, a short, and a long—the last "long" dying out far behind us. (I loved the sound of train whistles and knew all the signals by heart.) Now, with bells clanging and steam spraying out along the platform, we slid to a halt in front of the depot. A sign above the front window said SHAFTER. The milepost next to the track said No. 766.

The train had barely stopped when the porter swung down off the steps and placed a small step stool on the platform, setting my bag down beside it. He gave me his hand and helped me down. I noticed there were no other passengers, either getting on or getting off.

I stood blinking against the glare of the sun, reflected off the windows of the depot, and trying to take in the scene around me. Where were all the people? For that matter, where were all the *buildings?* My mother's letters had described this place as being "out in the country" with "lots of space to roam around in." She was right, there, of course. The view (unobstructed by houses or much of anything else) was of "space," lots of it, and I supposed you *could* roam around in it—if you liked hiking through sagebrush!

Picking up my suitcase and shading my eyes, I looked down the length of the train and spotted the baggage truck, a high, flat-bedded wagon, being pulled up to the door of the baggage car by my father in his "working clothes"— white shirt with garters around the sleeves, black vest, and matching trousers. The door opened and he was handed down a green and white Schwinn bicycle (my proudest possession, for which I had slaved a whole summer in Mrs. Mumson's boardinghouse), my grandmother's little camel-back trunk with the leather straps nearly worn through, now holding everything that would not fit in my small suitcase, and two large animal crates containing my dogs. I reflected on the fact that the baggage truck now being pulled away from the train contained all my worldly goods, with the exception of the clothes on my back and a few more in my suitcase. I was traveling light, merely because I didn't have much to begin with.

As soon as the wagon was pulled clear, I heard Mr. Sampson, at the end of the train crying, "Bo-WARD!" and saw him swinging a lantern in a "highball" to the engineer. Two short blasts from the whistle: woop, woop, told him that the "hogger" (what trainmen call an engineer) had read his signal to go. The brake was released and the engine, belching out a great plume of black smoke, lurched forward. When the dining car passed me, I saw Rafe's big smiling face in the open doorway. I waved and shouted, "THANK YOU!"

In my wildest dreams I would never have imagined that the next time I saw Rafe he would be risking his own neck to save mine!

CHAPTER TWO

Living in a Depot

Where in God's green Earth was I? Or rather, where in God's *brown* Earth? There was precious little *green* to be seen anywhere. Standing there on the platform I pictured myself as a real-life Dorothy in *The Wizard of Oz,* who had somehow got it backward. Dorothy had managed to go from her home in the grim black-and-white landscape of Kansas to the Emerald City of Oz, in living Technicolor. Conversely, from *my* home in the Emerald City of Sacramento, with its parks and trees and gardens, I had been blown into a desolate land of sand and sagebrush. I had never seen Kansas, but Nevada *had* to be worse! Now that the train had pulled out, I was able to see what lay on the other side of the tracks. A few crude buildings constructed of railroad ties, which I assumed were houses, were randomly strewn about the landscape (there were no roads or streets), each with its own outhouse in back. A larger building, directly across the tracks from where I stood, had a sign above the door:

GENERAL STORE AND U.S. POST OFFICE

The roof seemed to slope in all directions and looked as if it might not withstand another winter. The building itself looked to have been built in several sections or stages, with no particular plan in mind, and I figured that it catered to more activities than just the two listed on the sign. Later on, I would see that it also housed a sort of cafe (a counter with four stools where you could order bacon and eggs, or a sandwich, if you had the nerve), and—to my delight!—a pool table. I would find, too, that the rear portion of the building was devoted to living quarters for Joe Thomas, storekeeper and postmaster, his wife, and two children.

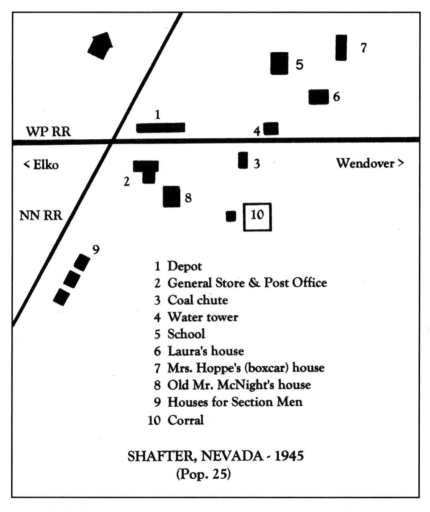

1 Depot
2 General Store & Post Office
3 Coal chute
4 Water tower
5 School
6 Laura's house
7 Mrs. Hoppe's (boxcar) house
8 Old Mr. McNight's house
9 Houses for Section Men
10 Corral

SHAFTER, NEVADA - 1945
(Pop. 25)

Map of Shafter, Nevada, in 1945

A woman came out of the General Store and Post Office, pausing in the doorway to wipe her hands on a grimy apron partly covering a faded cotton blouse and skirt, with the hem hanging loose along one side. She was wearing sneakers without socks and rolling a toothpick around in her mouth. The ribbons on my straw hat fluttered in the breeze. I looked down at my little seersucker suit and white open-toed shoes and decided that I was definitely over-dressed for the Great American Desert. The woman regarded me for a moment with no more than passing curiosity, then walked back inside.

The most imposing structures in view were the water tower and coal chute, located on either side of the track, only a short distance north of the depot. My father had told me these were the reason for Shafter's existence. Steam trains, whether freight or passenger, could not operate without coal and water, so tiny communities sprang up around the water towers and coal chutes.

What in the world had persuaded my mother to move to this God-forsaken place? It was not for love of my father, surely. In fact, they always seemed to get along better when living apart. A year ago Daddy had written about a job that she could have with another railroad, the Nevada Northern, whose tracks crossed the Western Pacific tracks right here at Shafter. The Nevada Northern was looking for someone to walk down the tracks each morning and count and record the numbers on the boxcars that would be dropped on the siding each night. It wasn't hard work, he explained, but it would require her to live here, of course. It was an opportunity to make some extra money, maybe get a little bit ahead, he argued. So, after thinking it over, she had decided to do it. Her modest little dressmaking business in Sacramento barely paid the rent, and now that my sister had married her Army Air Corps lieutenant and moved to Texas, there was only one other person to be considered. Me.

I was sure it wasn't the money, although that was certainly an inducement. My mother had nearly always been poor, and she had worked hard all her life, with little to show for her efforts. I knew she longed for beautiful things, a nice home, and an easier time of it. My father had been a disappointment in that regard, except for the early days of their marriage when he was a stockbroker in San Francisco. But that was before 1929, when it all came crashing down.

No, it wasn't just the little extra money this job would bring in, I was sure. There was something else. And then I thought I knew what it was.

After the Japanese, regardless of citizenship, had been evacuated from West Coast cities where they were perceived to be a threat to national security during the war, signs began appearing in and around Sacramento:

NOW THAT WE GOT THE JAPS OUT OF CALIFORNIA, LET'S GET THE GERMANS OUT, TOO!

My mother was German, and worried that she might be evacuated. She was a U.S. citizen, of course, but so were a good many of the Japanese being uprooted and unceremoniously sent off to "relocation camps." Even with the war winding down, following Italy's surrender two years ago, she could never be sure that someone wouldn't start rounding up the Germans. I knew she must have been greatly relieved when Germany surrendered, just last month, but by then she was already here, in an "exile" of her own making. After years of worrying about being evacuated, my mother had simply "evacuated" herself.

And me along with her.

Well, I was here, and there wasn't much I could do about it. All my bridges were burned. I could run away, but where would I go? And it would break my father's heart, not to mention the way my mother would make him suffer. (*This is all your fault, George!*)

I suddenly remembered my dogs, Lucky and Lucy, probably panting with thirst in those hot crates. I hurried toward the baggage room where my father was taking them.

"Hullo there, Punkin!"

I really *was* glad to see my father. The last time I saw him was at my sister's wedding in Sacramento, two years ago. She was married in the Catholic Church because her fiancé was "a mackerel snapper," as my father called Catholics who ate fish on Friday. He also quite irreverently observed, in a loud stage whisper during the ceremony, that the priest had forgotten to take off his bathrobe. My sister was furious.

"Hello, Daddy!"

It seemed to me that he had grown older in the months since I last saw him, and I tried to remember when his sandy hair had begun turning white. Still, he was a good looking man for his age, which was fifty-three. I was born when he was nearly forty, making him somewhat older than the fathers of other girls I knew. Now I began to wonder if it was the strain of having my mother here that was turning his hair white.

Where was my mother, anyway?

"Evelyn!"

The voice came from behind me, and when I turned around I saw her. She was hurrying along the tracks that crossed those of the Western Pacific. She was carrying a clipboard and the attached pages were flapping in the breeze as she trotted toward the depot. In contrast to my father, my mother seemed to have grown younger since I last saw her. The dark-brown hair, not yet beginning to gray, was worn in an attractive upsweep with a cluster of curls in the front. She was wearing a pink wool skirt and sweater (my mother was always cold, even on a hot day), and her cheeks seemed to glow with the same shade of pink.

"Hello, Mommy."

"I saw the train come in, but I had to finish counting the cars." Turning to my father she said, "Twenty-one today, Paddy."

"That's quite a number, Rosie."

So, they're getting along all right. That's a blessing, anyhow.

"Well, honey, did you have a good trip? The train was terribly late, wasn't it?"

"Yes."

"Did you have breakfast? Are you hungry?"

"No, I had breakfast . . . By the way, Daddy, some people on the train said to say hello to you."

"Oh? Who was that?"

"Mr. Sampson, the conductor, and—"

"So, Jack Sampson was on that train, was he?"

"Yes. He let me sleep in a berth last night."

"Good old Jack!" *I could see him mentally opening the ledger and deducting something from what good old Jack owed him.*

"And a big black man from the dining car, called Rafe. He and the crew arranged for me to have dinner last night and breakfast this morning, too," and now I looked accusingly at my mother, "even though I didn't have any *money!*"

Before my mother could react, my father said, "Always liked that fellow, Rafe. Reminds me of the great Jack Johnson! . . . Have I told you how I used to spar with Jack Johnson?"

Of course he had told me. I'd heard all Daddy's stories a hundred times, but I loved the way he told them. "No, I don't think so. Who was Jack Johnson?"

"A big man, like Rafe. They treated him badly because he was a Negro, and white men didn't want to see a black man as Heavyweight Champion of the World. It was shameful. People rioted when he won a fight against a white boxer. I was just a young sprout, still in college, but I was on the boxing team and I knew how to fight pretty well, so I applied for a job as one of the sparring partners to Jack Johnson. Well, sir, that man weighed about twice what I did. They called him the 'Galveston Giant,' and he was a champion, all right! Once he knocked me out cold, then came over and apologized for hitting me so hard. I was tickled pink to see him win the 'Fight of the Century' in 1910, when he beat—"

"Daddy," interrupted my mother. "Don't you think we'd better let Evelyn settle in, and not keep her standing here all day? I want to show her the room I've fixed up for her!" (My mother had heard all Daddy's stories a hundred times, too.)

"Yes, sure. I'll uncrate the pups, there, and give them some water, then take them outside so they can—"

"Fine," said my mother, hooking her arm through mine. "Let's go in through the office, Evelyn."

Without even seeing it, I knew the layout of the place. They were all alike, those Western Pacific depots, only varying a little in size, depending on the community they served. Everything was under one roof. The office would be in front, with windows that looked out in three directions so an operator could see everything on the tracks at once. On one side was the baggage room with big double doors and a small waiting room with hard wooden benches and a water cooler. On the other side, the agent's quarters. My father was the agent here in Shafter, working second trick (or shift), from 4:00 p.m. to midnight. The office had to be open twenty-four hours a day, so there would be two more operators, probably living in those houses made of railroad ties across the track.

I followed my mother into the office, where I noticed a girl with bright red hair sitting at the desk with her back to us. She had earphones on, and I knew she was busy receiving orders for the next train. I looked questioningly at my mother.

"That's Jean McNight," my mother whispered. "Two of the operators here are women. Both of them redheads! But with the manpower shortage, the railroads have no choice . . . Jean is married to Orvy McNight, the water tower operator, and the less said about *him,* the better. They're both very common," she sniffed. The worst thing my mother could say about anybody was that they were "common" or "coarse."

We had reached the door leading to the agent's quarters. Once inside, I could have found my way around in the dark. On the left of the narrow hallway was a fair-sized bedroom, looking out onto the "garden" in the back. My mother had told me about her attempts—mostly futile—to make a few things grow in soil that was more sand than anything else. Across the hall was a very small bedroom whose only window looked out onto the railroad track.

My mother stepped into the small room and threw her arms open wide. "Well, I promised you a room of your own, and here it is! What do you think?"

She had outdone herself. As an aspiring artist, some of her landscapes weren't too bad, I will admit. But everyone thought her portraits were God-awful. In this room she had painted a mural depicting the sun coming up over the mountains to the east, and on the opposite wall, a scene to resemble a full moon setting over the desert to the west. She had even painted the wooden floor a lush green. (I suppose she thought I'd miss having a lawn.) On the ceiling she had painted "stars" in a luminous silver paint.

"When you turn out the lights, the stars shine in the dark!" she said proudly. I knew that "turning out the lights" meant extinguishing the kerosene lamp on the wall above the bed.

Before she left Sacramento she had traded in her electric sewing machine for an old-fashioned treadle type. Since then she must have spent every waking hour—when she wasn't counting Nevada Northern boxcars—decorating this room. On the single iron bed, which she had painted teal blue, was a flowered chintz bedspread with matching ruffled pillow shams. A small slipper chair, in the same chintz, occupied one corner and pink gauzy curtains hung at the window. A combination washstand and dresser stood under the window, with a ceramic basin and pitcher for washing, either with cold water or with water heated on the stove in the kitchen. She had painted blue forget-me-nots on the white pitcher and basin.

"And if you have to get up ..." She was reaching under the bed to bring out a porcelain chamber pot. There were blue forget-me-nots on that, too.

Now she was pointing out the bookcases along the short wall. "Daddy made these for you. I put all your favorite books in them, plus some others that I bought in a used bookstore in Elko. I know how you like to read, and there's no library here." She didn't have to tell me ... *No library, no municipal swimming pool, no skating rink, no movie theaters ...* I turned to the bookcases and pretended to be studying the names on the spines of the books. I didn't want her to see the look on my face. "I thought you could display your Storybook Doll collection there, too. You did bring them, didn't you?"

"Sure. They're in my trunk."

"Oh, yes, your grandmother's trunk! I've got an idea for that, too. I thought we could paint it a gay color—I've got lots of paint left over—and decorate it with flowers." *More blue forget-me-nots.*

I was ashamed of feeling the way I did. No one would ever accuse my mother of not *trying!* The trouble was, she tried too *hard,* she always failed, and it made you feel sorry for her. My whole life, the overwhelming emotion I had for her was pity. She aspired to being a really good artist and sell her paintings, but no one would buy them. Once she had an idea for starting a business that involved women coming to our house for a "color analysis," where, for a fee, she would drape swatches of fabrics over a lady's shoulder and tell her which colors she looked best in. She put up notices all around town about the "Grand Opening of Rosalie's Color Analysis Studio." But nobody came. Another time she answered an ad in the newspaper for an illustrator of children's books and met with the lady who was going to write them. She worked day and night on drawings and watercolor sketches (which were poor imitations of Beatrix Potter, I thought), but the book was never published. She wanted to become a dress designer, and started making her own patterns, but nobody bought them. She even tried writing articles and stories for magazines, but never sold any. The one thing she could do moderately well was sew, but she got into such rows with her dressmaking customers that most of them stopped coming after a while.

She was a good mother, in spite of her Teutonic stubbornness—unselfish and generous. On several occasions, when my sister or I needed a dress to wear to a party, she had cut up one of her own to make it for us. She did things for my sister and me out of love for us. And she wanted to be loved in return. Ironically, the only person who really loved her was my father. And she couldn't love *him.*

Oh, why did I find it so hard to love my mother? It was easy to love my father. Everybody did (except my mother). He was easygoing and fun to be with. But not when he was drunk, of course. Then he became surly and argumentative, but my sister and I adored him, nonetheless.

Now she was waiting to hear what I thought of my new room, which she had tried so hard to make attractive for me. "It's . . . beautiful, Mommy." If I didn't get out of there in the next two minutes, I was afraid I would break down and tell her what I *really* thought—that I just wanted to go *home*. But where was that?

"Can I see the rest of the place?"

We walked down the hallway, passing the open door to the bigger bedroom with the double bed. I could not imagine my parents in bed together. I thought of my friend, Margie Riley, whose parents were like a couple of middle-aged high school sweethearts. On weekends they rarely got up before noon, and there was always a houseful of noisy children and their friends, all bounding in to sit on the parents' bed and read the funny papers while the grownups drank coffee and did the crossword puzzles. I envied my friend Margie for living in a house that rang with joy and laughter.

At the end of the hallway was a replica of every kitchen in every place my father had lived since I could remember. It had a big steel sink with a single tap—only once had I seen both cold *and* hot water taps—attached to the wall looking out onto the back yard, and a black wood-burning cookstove, opposite, where a teakettle was simmering, making the kitchen hot and steamy. The back door separated the sink from the end wall. In the corner there was a wooden icebox with two small doors in the front and a hinged, tin-lined compartment at the top, which held a block of ice. Next to the icebox was a kitchen table with four straight-backed chairs around it, and a coal oil lamp with a tall glass chimney sitting in the middle. Only one thing made this kitchen different from all the others I'd seen. Small chintz-covered cushions that matched my bedspread were tied onto the straight-backed chairs with little chintz bows.

My mother was pouring boiling water into a pot and inviting me to go and sit in the living room while she made tea. Relieved to get out of the overheated kitchen, I walked across the hall, where I was glad to see some familiar furniture from our house in Sacramento—a red frieze sofa and a couple of overstuffed chairs in cut velvet—that gave the place a homey look. The trouble was, it also made me homesick. Some of my mother's paintings hung on the otherwise bare walls, and I winced at seeing one of the God-awful portraits of me. (I always had to "sit" for her because she couldn't get anyone else. My sister flatly refused.)

"Now, isn't this nice?" My mother came into the living room carrying a tray that held the teapot, cups and saucers, a pitcher of milk, and a plateful of cookies. I knew what her cookies were like, so I told her I was still full from breakfast.

We were going to have to make some arrangement about the cooking here. My mother was the world's worst cook. She preferred to paint. But that was all right with me because I had become quite a good cook myself and had even done the cooking at Mrs. Mumson's boardinghouse when I worked there. I'd brought along a bunch of the "wartime recipes" that I had collected from Miss Kitchen's column in the Sacramento newspaper, too. Some of them— though admittedly not all—had become favorites at the boardinghouse. My curried oysters met with resistance, as did the ice cream I made from beets because I didn't have any strawberries. Well, that was really Miss Kitchen's fault. She encouraged inventiveness in the wartime cook.

My mother was pointing out the only piece of furniture in the living room that I did not recognize as being from our house in Sacramento. It was a wind-up Victrola in a tall wooden cabinet with shelves below, holding a dozen or more phonograph records in paper jackets.

"We can have music in the evenings," she was saying, while pouring the tea. "You can practice your dancing. Did you bring your ballet slippers?"

"Yes, and my tap shoes, too." *A fat lot of good they'd be out here! Five years at Miss Elizabeth's dance studio in Sacramento were down the drain!*

I was suddenly filled with despair. My sister and I had visited our father over the years in a dozen odd little burgs like this one. But in those days it was *fun*. We had laughed at the lack of amenities and always found something to do, even if it was only going fishing along the river and hooking nothing but the seat of our pants in our attempts at fly-casting. Back then, it was a vacation and we knew it was only for a week or a month at a time. This was beginning to have the grim feel of *permanence* about it! Oh, why hadn't they let me stay in Sacramento with Mrs. Todd a while longer? I'd be going into the eighth grade in September. My second year in junior high school.

School! Where was I going to go to school?

I needed to talk to Daddy. If anyone would understand how I felt, it was my father. "I think I'd better go and see how Daddy is doing with Lucky and Lucy . . . Is there anything for them to eat?"

"I saved some scraps from last night. And Daddy keeps a bag of dog biscuits in the baggage room for Moocher."

"Who?"

"A big brown dog that comes around every day for a handout. You'll see him."

I went out the back door and hurried along the wooden walkway behind the depot, passing the usual galvanized tubs hanging on the outside wall in three sizes. The two smaller ones I knew were for washing and rinsing clothes. There was a washboard hanging between them. The biggest of the three would be brought in and set on the kitchen floor, to be filled with water heated on the stove. We would each have a bath at least once a week. The outhouse was down a path to the right, only a short distance away. I smelled it before I saw it.

I found Daddy and my two dogs behind the baggage room, along with a big brown mutt "mooching" dog biscuits.

"There you are, Punkin! How do you like the room your mother fixed up for you?"

"It's fine . . . Whose dog is that?"

"Nobody's. But Joe Thomas lets him sleep in the store at night. And we all feed him. He's old, and pretty nearly deaf.

I just hope he doesn't go for a walk on the railroad track one day and get hit by a train. Even old Mr. McNight can't recall how long he's been here or where he came from."

The redhead I had seen looked too young to be married to "old" Mr. McNight. "You mean the husband of the girl in the office?"

"Oh, no. Her father-in-law. Jean's married to his son, Orvy, the water tower operator. Old Mr. McNight operates the coal chute . . . All right, now, Moocher! You've had enough. Go lie down." The dog paid no attention. "Can't hear me, poor old fella."

Lucy came bounding up and put her big soft paws on my shoulders. Standing on her hind legs, she was nearly as tall as I was. I patted her on the back.

"That dog looks like nothing I've ever seen before," said my father, shaking his head.

Big, dumb Lucy looked like nothing I'd ever seen before, either. And that included Lucky, her mother, a little terrier mix of some kind, smart as a whip and nearly all white. Lucy was almost all black and had long curly fur. Her adoring eyes were almost hidden by the hair hanging over them.

"Lucky must have taken a stroll with a Russian wolfhound one night," my father chuckled.

"Daddy . . . I was wondering . . ."

"Yes?"

"Do I have to stay here all the time?" Shading my eyes, I scanned the horizon for any sign of a school building. "I mean, where will I go to school?"

"Oh, there's a school here. I'll show you. We'll take a walk over there one day."

So, there was a school, after all. That just about doomed my chances of going back to Sacramento any time soon.

"We have a schoolmarm, too."

"What, just one?" Last year, in seventh grade at Sutter Junior High, we had a different teacher for each subject.

"Well, it's . . . a very small school." That would turn out to be the understatement of the year.

"How many kids?" It occurred to me that I hadn't seen any young people at all.

"Well, let me see. The Thomases have two—Donald and Betsy. And Mrs. Hoppe has two. That's four. And there may be—"

"Who's Mrs. Hoppe?"

"The schoolmarm. She and Mr. Hoppe and their two girls live in a boxcar across the way."

"In a *boxcar!*"

"Well, in order to attract a teacher, the town had to provide a place for one to live, so the W.P. donated a boxcar, and we cut windows and doors in it. This was a few years ago, and she's been there ever since. Guess she likes it."

I was almost afraid to ask. "What's she like, this Mrs. Hoppe?"

My father grinned. "Well . . . I think she's blind as a bat and twice as ugly! But that's only one man's opinion."

"You mean she can't *see?* How does she teach *school?*"

"Oh, she can see a little bit. Enough to walk around without falling down—although she does bump into things occasionally. And when she comes into the office for a Railway Express package, now and again, I notice she has to put the waybill right up to her nose to read it."

"You said there were other kids . . . How old are they?"

He thought a moment before answering. "I'm not sure, but I think the Thomas boy, Donald, is going into the fourth grade this year, and his sister, Betsy, will be in the sixth."

That would make her two years behind me. "And Mrs. Hoppe's girls?" I asked hopefully.

"Oh, they're younger, and only a year apart. Dorothy's going to be in the second grade, she told me, and Violet is just starting school this year."

"And that's *all?*"

"Well, as I said, there may be one or two more. I think a couple of the Mexican section men are married, and one has a little girl about six."

"So this, what's her name? Betsy?—is the only kid even *close* to my age?"

"That's about right."

I was starting to panic. "Daddy . . . couldn't I go back to Sacramento and stay with Mrs. Todd during the school year? And come back here in the summer?"

"Well, honey, that's something you should take up with your mother, if you decide that's what you want to do. But I'd wait a bit, if I were you. Sometimes we just need to make the best of things."

"Make the best of things . . ." I repeated dully. *How in the world was I supposed to do that?*

"Did I ever tell you about Lord D'Anjou?"

I thought I knew all my father's stories, but I didn't recall this one. "Lord who?"

"D'Anjou. You know, like the pear."

My grandfather, George (alias Lord D'Anjou) Smith

"Oh. What about him?"

"Sit down over here in the shade, and I'll tell you."

I sat down on a step shaded by the overhanging roof of the baggage room, and Lucy put her big hairy head in my lap.

"Well, sir . . . my father was a young man just out of college, facing a dull career in a small-town bank in St. Cloud, Minnesota, with his stuffy old man—my grandfather—who owned the bank. *His* name was Joseph Gaylord Smith. My father's name was *George* Gaylord Smith, and he hit upon a plan to have a little fun. He went down to the courthouse and had his name legally changed to Lord D'Anjou. He just cut 'Gaylord' in half to make 'Lord,' you see, then added 'D'Anjou' as a last name. Next, he brushed up on his French, and before anyone knew what he was doing, he'd taken all the money out of his account at the bank and sailed off to Europe as the dashing Lord D'Anjou."

"This was your father?"

"That's right. And your grandfather."

"But why did he do that?"

"Well, I guess he was feeling a little restless and wanted to live someplace more exciting for a while."

"So, what happened?"

"It seems he had such a good time in Paris that he spent a whole year there, sowing his wild oats, and one thing and another. But when his money ran out, he had to go home to Minnesota and ask for his old job back. Now, *believe you me,* his father wasn't happy about the way his son had acted, and he told him there was *no* 'Lord D'Anjou' on the payroll! He said, 'If you want to work in my bank, you go down to the courthouse and change your name back to 'George Smith.' And my father had to do it because he needed a job."

I suddenly remembered something. "Wait a minute. Is this part of the story about three drops of royal blood?"

"That's right. My father got kind of carried away with thinking of himself as a lord and decided that he must have *three* drops of royal blood in him. Don't ask me how he came up with that exact number, but he used to tell me that I had *two* drops of royal blood, and when you were born he said you had *one*. That's the last drop, you see, which makes *you* the last Lady D'Anjou!"

"Whatever made him think of a name like D'Anjou?"

"Well, he wanted something that sounded French, but wasn't too hard to spell or pronounce . . . And he happened to be eating a pear at the time."

"Daddy! You made all this up, didn't you?"

"No, no. I've still got one of my father's calling cards in the name of Lord D'Anjou. He had a bunch of them printed up before he left. I can show it to you if you don't believe me." I knew that my father didn't lie, though he didn't mind embellishing the truth once in a while. But why had he told me this particular story now? I was silent, so he said, "My father had to go back to his boring old job at the bank in a small town he didn't like very much, either. But he eventually got used to it. The moral of the story, sweetheart, is that sometimes we just need to make the best of things."

That night, as I lay in my little teal-blue iron bed and stared up at those ridiculous "stars" on the ceiling, I wept silently—for my poor mother, who tried too hard and always failed and made you feel sorry for her, and for myself, the doomed last Lady D'Anjou.

CHAPTER THREE

Making the Best of Things

The next morning I awakened to the sun streaming in through the gauzy pink curtains at my window. I had been dreaming that I was Shirley Temple in one of those "little princess" movies, where she wakes up to find that her once-shabby room has been luxuriously redecorated during the night by an exotic benefactor, played by Cesar Romero. But it was not Cesar Romero who was pawing at my arm to wake me, it was Lucy.

Lucky was still curled up in the chintz-covered slipper chair, but Lucy was eager for the day to begin, and maybe to find a jackrabbit to chase. I wished I were that easily entertained. What in the world was I going to do here?

I sat up in bed and looked around. All right, things could be worse. I would just have to *find* things to do. Sometime today I might get out my bike and do some exploring. Daddy had said there were Indian arrowheads by the hundreds scattered all over this area. I could start collecting the most attractive ones. I had already unpacked my Storybook Doll collection and installed it in the bookcase Daddy had built. For once my mother was right. They did look pretty, peeking out among the books. I was too old to play with dolls, of course, but these weren't dolls you "played" with. You just looked at them.

I was still awake the night before when Daddy came home, shortly after midnight when his shift in the office ended, and Laura, the other redhead my mother had mentioned, took over. Daddy had told me that I would like Laura Dembowski. She was not much older than I was, he said. Nineteen, or maybe twenty, the same age as my sister. But there the comparison ended, I figured. My mother had always accused my sister of being "selfish and bone-lazy," but Laura Dembowski worked. And her job was not an easy one.

At first, my father had been concerned about having a beautiful redhead, and only a "slip of a girl," as he called Laura, alone in the office at night, with rough trainmen coming and going at all hours. But he needn't have worried about her! She assured him that she was a "tough Texas lady—scared o' nuthin'," and then proved it with Orvy McNight, the water tower operator.

Orvy had taken to hanging around the office on Laura's shift, while his wife, Jean, was home sleeping and once he had made the mistake of patting Laura on the fanny. That time she told him in no uncertain terms—Daddy said she could also *swear* like a tough Texas lady!—to back off. But the next time he tried it, she threw an elbow into Orvy's ribs so hard that it knocked the wind out of him. He never tried it again.

I could smell bacon frying. That meant that Daddy was up and ready for his breakfast. Remembering yesterday and the breakfast Rafe had brought me on a tray in the Pullman car made me wish that I was still on the train, only headed back in the other direction, toward Sacramento. But what was the use of thinking about it? *Sometimes we just have to make the best of things, Daddy had said.*

It was going to be a hot day. I remember thinking that the water in the pitcher painted with the blue forget-me-nots must have been warmed by the sun as I washed my face at the washstand underneath the window. I put on a pair of sandals, shorts, and a blouse. I looked at my little seersucker suit now hanging in the small closet and decided sadly that I probably would never wear it again. Not out here in the Great American Desert.

Unpacking my suitcase the day before, I had come across my ration book, issued by the OPA, which stood for Office of Price Administration, one of the many "alphabet agencies" Mr. Roosevelt had created while he was president. It made me sad to think about poor Mr. Roosevelt. He had died two months ago, never seeing the end of the war, or

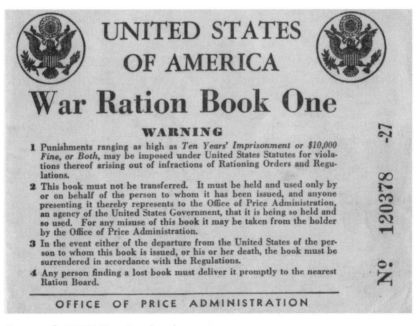

Cover of a WW II ration book

the creation of a United Nations, either, which had always been his fondest dream. To me, personally, his death had been a terrible loss. After all, he had been elected the year I was born, and I had never known any other president. I was not too sure about Mr. Truman. That is, whether I liked him or not. But if he could end the war I would love him. I would love *anyone* who could end this awful war!

I opened my ration book and counted the stamps inside. Still plenty of red ones (for meat and butter), green ones for canned goods, blue for coffee (I didn't drink coffee, but Mommy would be glad to have them, probably), and those gray ones called "spares." I never did figure out what those were for. You had to have a ration book if you wanted to buy food, shoes, gasoline, tires, or anything that was rationed. Recently, milk and dairy products had been taken off the list, which was good.

I found my mother standing over the stove in the kitchen, trying to turn sizzling strips of bacon in a heavy black iron skillet with one hand and take toast out of the oven with the other. A tall enameled coffee pot simmered at the back. I took the long fork from her and poked at the bacon. "I remembered to bring my ration book," I said.

"Oh, you won't need it here, honey. Joe Thomas doesn't bother with them."

"He *doesn't?*" What kind of treason was this? For three years I had faithfully surrendered ration stamps for everything I bought, not to mention two years ago, when I did the cooking in the boardinghouse and had to keep track of *eight* ration books, including my own! "Why not?"

"Well, he says the government created rationing to keep

people from hoarding things, like coffee and canned goods, and buying up big quantities and causing shortages. But out here no one has enough money to buy more than they need, and sometimes not even that, so . . ." She shrugged her shoulders and seemed to imply that this was Nevada, where people made the rules and took the law into their own hands.

If that was so, it was going to take some getting used to.

"Hullo, Punkin! How'd you sleep?" My father came in through the kitchen door and scraped his stubbly chin against my cheek, making me wince. "Guess I'd better shave, eh?"

"Your breakfast is ready, Pad. You can shave later," my mother said in her usual authoritative way. With a wink at me, Daddy sat down at the table. My mother was already sliding his eggs and bacon onto a plate and piling fried potatoes along the side. "It's time I was going . . . Would you like to come along, Evelyn? It's really rather interesting."

For the moment it had slipped my mind that my mother had a job—and the ostensible reason for her (and my) being here—counting the Nevada Northern boxcars every morning. What I really wanted to do was sit down at the table with Daddy and eat a big breakfast of eggs, fried potatoes, and bacon, all smothered in ketchup just the way he would, but I thought it was more important to start off on the right foot with my mother.

I have to admit that I was sorry for my less-than-enthusiastic reaction to the way my mother had decorated my room. She was no Cesar Romero—no exotic benefactor who could magically transform a hovel into a room fit for a little princess! But she had *tried,* after all. And maybe she hadn't even noticed my lack of enthusiasm. It was not easy to hurt my mother's feelings (and I wouldn't, for the world). Even when her Color Analysis Studio was a complete failure and the children's book didn't get published, and nobody bought her paintings, was she discouraged? If so, she never showed it. Instead, she simply shrugged and said it "wasn't to be." In fact, she would be shocked to learn that I had ever felt sorry for her. She never seemed to feel sorry for *herself.* She believed that everything was an act of God and therefore inevitable. Things always turned out for the best.

"Sure. Can we take the dogs? They need a good walk after being in a cage all that time."

My mother and I with canine friends

So our little party of boxcar counters started off down the Nevada Northern tracks: my mother, walking briskly with her clipboard under her arm, my two dogs, with Moocher straggling behind, and me. Watching her striding along, I decided that my mother would have made a good drill sergeant. She had that Teutonic bearing, that purposeful, no-nonsense demeanor. I had a hard time keeping up with her.

My father had been right. The work was not hard. When you came to the first boxcar, you wrote #1 on the tally sheet and next to it you recorded the number stenciled on the side of the car. Then you went to #2, and so on down the line. A cinch in warm or even hot weather, which never bothered my mother, but how would she like tramping along here in the wintertime? Anything below sixty degrees was cold in her view. On the map it said Shafter was in a "high desert." At more than a mile above sea level, it snowed here, too.

Rounding the end of the last boxcar, I was surprised to see a little girl with dark skin and big brown eyes staring at us from a short distance away.

"Who's that?"

Glancing up from her clipboard, my mother said, "Oh, she probably belongs to one of the section men—the crew that repairs the track."

"Where does she live?"

"In one of those houses down there, I imagine." She was pointing toward some shabby buildings along the Nevada Northern tracks, farther down.

"Do they work for the Nevada Northern?"

"No, they're with the Western Pacific. Well, let's—"

"Why don't they live closer in?"

"Well, the townspeople wouldn't want them living right next *door.*"

My mother's beliefs were an odd mixture of religion and reality. She would be the first to say that all God's children were equal in His sight, but you wouldn't want to live next door to most of them!

"You mean stuck-up folks like us, who live in a train depot, and Mrs. Hoppe, who lives in a boxcar, and that woman I saw yesterday in front of the store who looks like something out of 'Tobacco Road?' You mean townspeople like *that?*"

"There's no need to be rude," my mother snapped.

Now you've done it. Here I was, trying to start off on a new tack with her, and already I was making her angry. I said I was sorry, then turned my attention back to the little girl. She might be the six-year-old that my father thought would be starting school this year. If so, I wondered if she spoke English. I moved a few steps closer to her. She didn't run away so I said, "Do you speak English?

She shook her head.

I summoned up the few words in Spanish that I knew, and said, "Donde vive usted?"

The little girl pointed to the first house down the track.

My mother was surprised. "Where did you learn to speak Spanish?"

"Oh, I palled around with a couple of girls last year in junior high school. They were from Guatemala."

My mother's disapproval was evident from her tight-lipped "Hmph."

"Cómo . . . How do you say, 'what's your name?' Let's see . . . Su nombre?" I said hopefully. I knew I was making a hash of it, but she seemed to understand.

"Juanita," she said. "Pero, me llamo Nita."

"Muy bien, Nita! Yo soy Evelina, and this . . ." (pointing to my mother) "es mi madre, Rosita."

My mother might have been a snob but she liked children, and I caught her smiling at the little girl and even nodding when I called her "Rosita."

"Do you go to school? . . . Escuela?"

Nita shook her head.

How to ask her if she would be going in the fall? "En . . . Septiembre?"

She shrugged.

"Cuántos años tiene?"

"Seis."

"She's six years old. She should be going to school this year."

"How is she supposed to go to school if she doesn't understand English?"

It was a good question. "Does Mrs. Hoppe speak any Spanish?"

"With a half-dozen children in grades one through eight, how is she supposed to teach one child in Spanish?"

"I wonder if her mother speaks any English." It was a long shot, but I asked it, anyway. "Nita, habla Inglés, su madre?"

Another shrug. That might mean her mother spoke a little English.

"Está en casa, su madre?"

"Sí."

"Ahora?"

"Sí."

I reached out, and Nita put her small hand into mine. "Vamos, muchacha," I said, and we set off in the opposite direction.

"Where are you going?" There was a note of alarm in my mother's voice.

"I'm going to see Nita's mother."

"You mean . . . in one of those houses?"

"Yes. Why don't you go back, Mommy, and take the dogs with you. I won't be long, I promise."

And so the little party of boxcar counters split up, my mother shaking her head disapprovingly, but calling the dogs to follow her home. Lucy and Moocher went trotting after her, but Lucky stuck close to me, so the three of us—Nita, Lucky, and I—went to see Señora Hernandez. I came back about an hour later with a new purpose in life.

Nita's mother was a pretty woman, probably in her mid-twenties, with raven hair and sparkling brown eyes. The house they lived in was little better than a shack, but it was immaculately clean. Señora Hernandez was overjoyed, and obviously flattered, that I should take the trouble to drop by and ask about her daughter's plans for school. She spoke a few words of English, but told me she couldn't read. I asked if she would let me teach Nita some English, and maybe teach both of them to read. She was almost overwhelmed by the suggestion. Would Señor Hernandez mind if I came here every day for an hour or so and brought some books with me? Oh, no, Señorita! But she would speak with him.

And so it was settled, without even consulting my parents. Every morning for the rest of the summer I walked down the tracks with my mother, but left her at the end of the line of boxcars, and went on to the Hernandez house with books, paper, and pencils. I taught Nita the alphabet and how to write her name. She was very bright and quick to learn. By September she could even read a little. And so could her mother.

It was gratifying to do what I could for these people who, as my father said, "didn't have our advantages." What advantages were those, I wondered, beside the fact that our forebears came from Europe instead of Mexico. But that fact alone seemed to make a lot of difference.

I was still having trouble finding enough to do. My arrowhead collection had soon grown to two boxes. Besides riding my bike I also walked a lot, picking up arrowheads and other Indian artifacts that I found in abundance on the desert floor. I never knew if the arrowheads were used to shoot game or people (on the map there was something called "Battle Mountain" not far from here). Some of the arrowheads were quite beautiful, being made of hard stone in several colors. The prettiest ones were shiny black, chipped on all sides, and made into a sharp point at one end with whatever tools they had back then. The dogs were in seventh heaven, scampering after whatever moved. The only thing that could outrun Lucky, who was "the fastest thing on four feet," as my father used to say, was a jackrabbit. Lucy didn't care to work that hard, so she stuck to ground squirrels, which disappeared down their holes after a short distance. Moocher, with his painful arthritic joints, only went so far with us before turning around and limping home.

Sometimes Daddy walked with us. Having him along always reminded me of one summer in northern California when we were walking to the river to fish. On the way he bent down to pick up Lucky's ball, which had rolled under a bush. A split second later I watched in horror as a rattlesnake struck him in the arm—*and held on!* Daddy reached into his fishing basket and pulled out his knife. He cut the snake loose and cut his arm, too, to let the venom drain out. He had me rip up his shirt and make a crude tourniquet to tie around his arm just above the elbow, so the poison wouldn't reach his heart. I was almost paralyzed with shock, and we had about a mile to walk back to his quarters in the train depot before we could get help. Sweat was pouring off his forehead, and he leaned heavily on my shoulder as he walked. I was sure my father was going to die, if not on the way home, then later. When we reached the depot, I wanted to run into town and tell someone to phone for a doctor, but he said he didn't need a doctor. What he needed was his bottle of whiskey in the kitchen cupboard.

For the next three days he lay in bed, seemingly at death's door. He looked horrible. His face swelled up and turned crimson, making his head look like a big, shiny balloon. Most of the time he didn't speak, and when he did, it didn't make any sense. At the end of the third day he sat up and asked if there was any more whiskey in the house. That's when I knew he was going to be all right.

That all happened in another little railroad town of a few hundred people in the wilds of northern California, but it was *civilization* compared to this! Some people had telephones and even cars. There was a doctor in a neighboring community and, about twenty-five miles away, a small hospital. That same year I broke my arm in two places and had to be taken to that hospital to have the bones set after I was bucked off a horse.

What if you had a medical emergency out here—if you broke a bone or had a heart attack or got bitten by a snake? The only way that I could see to get in and out of Shafter was by rail. That meant you would just have to wait for the next train to take you to a doctor or the nearest hospital, which was in Wendover, on the border with Utah, about forty miles up the line.

On one of our walks around Shafter Daddy said he would show me the school. I had seen pictures of old school buildings that were used in the last century, but I never expected to be enrolled in one! On first sight, I thought it was an old church. It had a small bell tower raised above the high, pitched roof, with a tarnished metal bell hanging in it, and two steps leading up to a double front door, with a window on each side. The whole building was only one room wide and one room deep, making it truly a "one-room school." I stood staring at it, recalling my father's earlier description: "Well, it's a very small school." Truer words were never spoken.

But I didn't need to think about it right now. There was still half a summer left before school started. Maybe there would be an earthquake or something, if we were lucky!

After seeing the school, we walked back to the depot, cutting through Laura's back yard. Laura's house was probably the best one in Shafter. It was built of real wood instead of railroad ties. Of course, there was no electricity or "inside plumbing" in her house, either, but being a "tough Texas lady" she didn't seem to mind. Jean McNight constantly complained to Orvy about the lack of amenities in their place—but what she expected him to do about it, I could never figure out.

My father had been correct when he predicted that I would like Laura Dembowski. She liked me, too, and called me "Slim." She was the same age as my sister (twenty), but we got along much better. I loved my sister, of course, but I admired Laura, not only for her fearlessness, but for her beauty. Her hair was a deep mahogany red. Not like Jean's, which was a kind of fake ginger color. Jean always wore dresses in the office, but Laura wore Levi's and cowboy boots. Except for Dale Evans, in the movies, I had never seen a woman in Levi's, much less boots! We became pals immediately, even though Laura was older and a married woman with a husband in the Army. She worked third trick (midnight to 8:00 a.m.) in the office, which meant she had to sleep part of the day, and didn't usually get up much before midafternoon. My father's shift began at 4:00 p.m., and I liked to spend the early part of the afternoon with him, practicing my Morse Code.

As the daughter of a telegrapher, I learned Morse Code almost as soon as I learned to read. Daddy had an extra telegraph key, or "bug," as they were called, and I would tap out messages for him, and he would send messages back to me. I could type just as well as my father on the office typewriter, too (we both used the hunt-and-peck system), and many times he let me write out the orders that would be handed up to the trains as they sped through the crossing.

My father's telegraph key, or "bug"

One copy would be for the fireman, who would crouch down low between the engine and the tender, hooking his arm through a wooden hoop with the engineer's orders attached, and another copy was for the conductor or brakeman in the caboose, who would grab his orders from a second hoop. Sometimes Daddy let me stand out on the platform, holding up the two hoops. But you had to do it just right, because if they missed their orders, the train would have to stop. Then an unhappy trainman would have to come into the office to get them, losing precious minutes off a schedule.

Some of the things that Laura and I did together were fun and exciting. We would "hop freights" either going north to Wendover, or south to Elko, riding at the end of the train in the caboose with the conductor and brakeman or

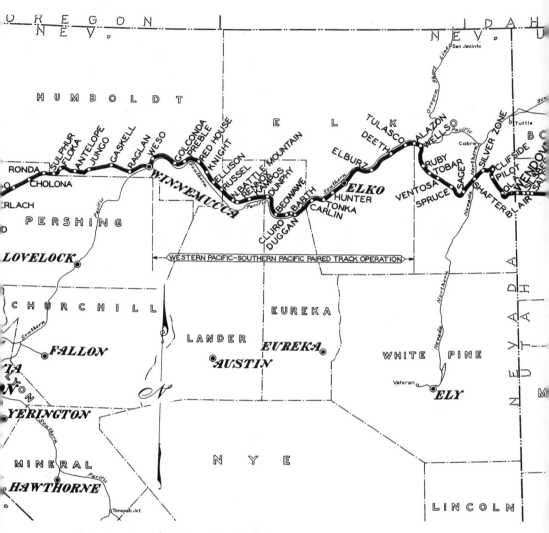

Route map of Western Pacific line

up front in the engine. Sometimes the engineer, if he had a sense of humor, would let us put on his and the fireman's caps and sit in their seats, while they stayed out of sight. The reaction of onlookers scattered along the track, seeing two girls running a 150-ton locomotive, was priceless!

Our favorite trainman was Mr. Parker, a young, good-looking conductor. I had the feeling that Mr. Parker was sweet on Laura. *Well, it was hard not to be. But Mr. Parker was wasting his time. Laura was only sweet on Johnny.* Her husband, Johnny Dembowski, was overseas somewhere. Laura kept a framed photograph of him by her bed, and I knew she missed him. The fact that Laura was married didn't stop Mr. Parker from hanging around her whenever he could. One time his caboose had a flat wheel, or something, and he arranged to park it on the siding at Shafter while he waited

A Western Pacific caboose

with the crippled car for a special crew to be sent out to fix it. *I think I know why it took a week for that crew to show up.* But for me, having the caboose in Shafter was like having a little house of my own for a week. It was the beginning of my lifelong love affair with cabooses. I spent hours dusting and sweeping—trainmen were notoriously bad housekeepers— and once I even washed the windows, which were always black with coal smoke from the engine, outside, and smoke from the pot-bellied stove, inside. Only, I forget to tell Mr. Parker what I had done, and the next time he went to throw the remains of a pot of stale coffee out the window, it was a disaster. The window was so clean that he had assumed it was open. I sneaked out the back door when I heard him growl, "Who washed that damned window?"

Once in a while Laura and I would take a train into Wendover to see a movie, being careful to get back to Shafter in time for her to go to work at midnight.

One night we didn't make it in time. *And we were lucky to make it at all.*

CHAPTER FOUR

Looking for Trouble

The first time I walked into the General Store and Post Office, it was like being in an old black-and-white movie about the Wild West. Once inside the squeaky screen door, the first thing you saw was the counter to your left, about eight feet long. On it was a scale that advertised "Honest Weight," and underneath, a glass case filled with such sundries as pipe tobacco, toothpaste, and patent medicines. Behind it, against the wall, were shelves going all the way up to the ceiling, stacked with canned goods. On the floor there were sacks and barrels of dried beans, peas, lentils, rice, and macaroni in different shapes and sizes. A couple of feet in front of the counter was a pot-bellied stove, the only heat in the place during the winter, I imagined. Straight ahead was a lunch counter with four stools where you could order something to eat, if you could weather the frosty looks from Mrs. Joe Thomas. She was supposedly the cook, but Grace Thomas made it clear that she didn't like being called upon to do any cooking! To the right was a battered upright piano and a round piano stool. In the middle of the room, with barely enough space to swing a cue, was a pool table. A rack of pool cues hung on the wall next to the window at the front of the store, with a sign tacked up over it:

NO SWEARING OR LOUD TALK
NO TRICK SHOTS. IF YOU SCRATCH
THE TABLE, YOU PAY FOR IT

A large coal-oil lamp hung over the middle of the pool table, but it was not the only light in the place. There was a generator behind the store (the only one in town) that produced electricity for the meat locker and a few electric lights. There was even a radio, which you could hear playing sometimes in the living quarters at the back.

Outside, the sign over the front door advertised a U.S. Post Office, in addition to a General Store, but it was not like any other post office I had ever seen. There were no numbered metal boxes with keys or combination locks. Joe Thomas simply sorted whatever mail was contained in a blue drawstring bag that was thrown off the morning train and kept it under the counter until you went in and asked for it. He also sold stamps and put any outgoing mail in the bag, which left again on the next train. That seemed to pretty well sum up his duties as the postmaster of Shafter.

My mother had tried to get me interested in the Thomases' young daughter, Betsy, as a playmate, believing that Laura Dembowski was too mature for me to be palling around with, and even considered her a bad influence because of her "language." Betsy Thomas was a plump little round-faced girl with "dishwater blonde" hair worn in pigtails. Now that I was a teenager, I considered myself much too sophisticated to take an interest in the activities of an eleven-year-old—Betsy still played with *dolls*—and especially one who had been born and raised in this mud hole! Her nine-year-old brother, Donald, was a brat of the first water, whose only interest seemed to be capturing creepy-crawly things that he found out on the desert and scaring people with them.

Obviously, without Laura Dembowski I would have no friends at all. I went to the General Store and Post Office every day, supposedly to buy groceries and pick up the mail, but that wasn't all. I really went there to play pool. At first I wasn't very good, but after hours of daily practice—when my mother thought I was occupied with more wholesome activities, such as hunting for arrowheads or playing dolls with Betsy—my pool shots improved dramatically. Once in a while I persuaded Joe Thomas to play with me. Customers to the store were few and far between, and he seemed to have a lot of time to stand behind the counter with his arms folded across his chest, chewing on a toothpick. I liked having someone to play against, even if I was better than he was. After a few games he suggested playing for money— ten cents a game. I had my allowance in my pocket, so I decided to risk it. Two games later, I went home twenty cents richer.

The next day I was practicing my shots when one of the Mexican section crew came into the store to buy groceries and cigarillos. I caught him watching me with great interest, so I said, "Buenos días, Señor. Quiere usted jugar?" (I knew the Spanish word for *cards,* but I didn't know the word for *pool,* so I just left it at that: "Do you want to play?") At first the man hesitated, so I asked Joe Thomas if he thought it would be all right, and without taking the toothpick out of his mouth, Joe said, "Don't know why not." I think he was secretly hoping the guy would beat the socks off me. If so, he was disappointed. That afternoon I went home with more money in my pocket. A couple of days later the first man, whose name was Señor Gonzales, brought another member of the crew in with him and challenged me to a game. The stakes were upped to twenty-five cents. On Friday, which was the section men's payday, five of them showed up. And so it went, week after week. I knew I should not be taking the men's money for betting on pool games, but in my own mind I rationalized it as entertainment, and educational, too. The men laughed easily and loved to make fun of my Spanish (it *was* pretty bad). So I proposed that I should speak to them in English and they should speak to me in Spanish. That way, in addition to having fun, we would all be improving our language skills. And I never took money from Señor Hernandez, little Nita's father, who was the only one of the men with a family.

Naturally, I wouldn't expect my parents to see it quite the same way I did, and for that reason I thought it best to keep my newly acquired wealth a secret. So I hid an envelope full of cash at the back of my underwear drawer, knowing that if they ever found out what I was doing, they would kill me!

Only, I hadn't counted on God trying to do it for them! That was the day when I walked out of the store with a bag of groceries and saw a freight train standing on the track, taking on coal and water and blocking my way across to the depot. Looking up and down the length of the track I could see nothing but freight cars for a mile or more. The train was too long to walk around, and it was impossible to tell how soon this monster would get out of my way. It was getting late, and my mother would be wanting the groceries for supper.

Well, I had crawled under trains before, so . . .

I knew I had better not let my father see me doing it. It

was after 4:00, so he would be at work, but not necessarily looking out at the track. I slid the bag of groceries between the rails, halfway under the train, and then climbed in after it. Of course I was smart enough to crawl through at a point well ahead of the next set of wheels that would roll over me if the train should start up while I was under it. But that had never happened.

Until now.

To my horror, I felt a shuddering in the rails as the train began to move. I could see the far set of wheels coming closer, slowly at first, but picking up speed. Leaving the bag of groceries behind, I scrambled across the rocks between the rails, with the undercarriage of the car moving along only inches above my head, and then over the second rail to safety, just seconds before the big steel wheels rolled past the place where I had been. Except for a cut on my knee and a tear in my pants which I got from a sharp spike in the roadbed, I was shaken but unhurt.

I didn't have long to congratulate myself on how clever I'd been. A moment later I was grabbed roughly by the arm and pulled up to a standing position on the platform. I had never seen my father so angry. Still holding me firmly by the arm, he marched me into the office, where the look on my mother's face told me that she had seen me, too. She was about to unleash a good tongue-lashing, when she caught sight of the blood soaking through my pants.

"George! . . . She's hurt!"

Daddy sat me down in a chair and rolled up my pant leg. "It's only a cut, Mother. Nothing too serious. Get a basin of water and a towel, will you?"

For once, my mother did as she was told. When she got back with a basin of warm water, a washcloth, a package of bandages, and a bottle of iodine (*that, I knew, was going to sting like all get-out!*), Daddy was well into a lecture about just how BIG and DANGEROUS a TRAIN can be! But he could have saved his breath. Seeing tons of black iron and shiny steel passing within inches of my skull had brought *that* fact home to me better than he ever could. From that moment on, I would give trains a wide berth and not go looking for trouble.

At least that's what I planned to do.

For a while I stuck close to home, and even abandoned my moneymaking pool games. Now, when I went into the General Store and Post Office, I just bought groceries and picked up the mail. Laura and I had not "hopped a freight" for some time, in deference to my mother's wishes that I find something else to do. But eventually, boredom got the better of me and I decided to explore some places I had not been before. This time I took my bike and rode parallel to the railroad tracks, heading south in the direction of Elko. What I hoped to see that might be different, I couldn't say. It turned out to be only more of the same. Sand and sagebrush for mile upon endless mile. Until your eye reached the blue-green mountains in the distance, the land was so flat "it could slide under a gate," like parts of Texas, Laura said. But I had to admit that there was a kind of wild beauty to the landscape, shimmering with waves of heat rising up from the desert floor, here and there dotted with scrubby patches of pink and yellow wildflowers.

I had packed a lunch and filled a canteen with water,

which hung over the handlebars of my bike. I also had a sack of dog biscuits in the basket for Lucky and Lucy. Moocher had taken one look at our little party setting off on what looked like a long trek and gone back to sleep in the shade of the baggage room. *As things turned out, he showed more sense than any of us.*

I don't know how far I had gone before I came to a wide dry wash or old riverbed. The railroad tracks ran over it on a timber trestle, built a long time ago, by the looks of it. The arroyo was too deep and bumpy to cross with the bike, so I leaned it up against the earthen berm and scrambled up onto the bridge for a better view of what might be up ahead and to decide whether I wanted to go there. I called to the dogs to follow, and Lucky scrambled up after me, but Lucy lay down in the sand and put her big hairy head on her paws in a gesture of defiance.

"Okay, Lucy, you stay there and guard the bike." Fat lot of help *she'd* be!

And what was there to guard against, anyway? Cattle rustlers looking to steal a shiny, green and white Schwinn with prewar tires?

About a fourth of the way across the bridge, I traced with my eye the long, snaking course of the dry wash off into the distance, ending up against the mountains. I wondered what had cut away that much sand and debris in its path, and then I remembered that there were sometimes flash floods in this part of the country. I'd heard stories about a wall of water that came crashing down out of the mountains, without warning, and in bright, clear weather, too. Weather like today.

Lucky was becoming agitated. She seemed to be listening to something, but I couldn't hear anything. I went on looking at the riverbed and thinking about flash floods. Then I did hear something, only faintly, like a far-off rumbling. And now I could feel it. A slight trembling of the railroad track on that ancient wooden trestle. There were earthquakes in this part of the country, too, I remembered. On a walk with my father one day, we had seen where the land had been split into a chasm several feet wide, the result of an earthquake at some time. Would this old bridge hold up in an earthquake? It looked almost ready to fall down by *itself!*

"Come on, Lucky, let's get off this thing." The far-off rumbling was closer now. Whether it was a flash flood or an earthquake made no particular difference at that moment. I reasoned that it would be safer to be on the ground at either end of the trestle. I was starting to walk back, in the direction we had come, when I looked up and saw the black smoke.

It wasn't a flash flood or an earthquake. *It was a train!*

I stopped dead, staring at the big black face of a locomotive, highballing along at top speed—maybe eighty-five miles an hour. Now Lucky was dancing up and down on her dainty white feet and pleading with little yips and yaps for me to *do something!* But what? I stood there thinking: this doesn't make any sense! I knew every train that was scheduled to pass along here every day, in both directions, and there was none scheduled for this time today, I was sure.

If it hadn't been for Lucky's wild barking, by now, I might have stood stock still and let the train run right over me. I had wasted precious minutes, frozen to the spot. *Now I had to think! I had to move—in one direction or another—but which way?* Trying to outrun a train is the act of a very foolish, or a very desperate, person. At the moment, I was both! I was closer to the end of the bridge the train was approaching, but trying to get back there before it reached the spot where I could safely slide down the earthen berm and off the trestle was a gamble. The other option, trying to get to the far end before the engine caught up with me, seemed almost impossible. I looked over the side and tried to estimate the distance to the ground, in case I had to jump. I have never been good at judging distances, and it might have been 30 feet or 130, or somewhere in between, but I knew that Lucky would be killed and I would break a lot of bones. (I remembered what a relatively short fall off the back of a horse had once given me: an arm broken in two places.)

I tried to estimate the width of the bridge and whether there would be room for the train to pass if I stayed where I was. I have walked that close to a train when it was standing still, but I figured that one moving at that speed would either blow me off the trestle or pull me under the wheels. I had no choice. I had to run. And, against all odds, I would try to outrun the train and make it to the other end ahead of it.

I gestured wildly in that direction. "Go, Lucky! RUN!"

She needed no further encouragement. My little dog ("the fastest thing on four feet," as my father called her) took off like the wind. And I followed.

It is not easy to run on railroad ties, especially knowing

that the slightest misstep will result in disaster. I knew the train was not far behind me now. The engineer had seen me and was signaling with a succession of short, frantic blasts on the whistle: woop, woop, woop, woop, woop, woop, which means "obstruction on the tracks"—and the obstruction was *me!* Then I heard the sickening screech of steel grinding against steel as he threw everything he had into stopping the train. But it wasn't enough. The engine shot by me in a cloud of smoke. Hot steam and sparks, flying out from under the wheels, burned my legs. The noise was almost deafening, but I had some hope of making it, now that the locomotive was past me.

Until I saw the signpost directly in front of me.

I remembered seeing one just like it on the other side of the track as I started across the trestle, but had paid no attention at the time. Now I was seeing this one clearly enough. It was a thick post with a wide square sign attached at the top. In big back letters it said:

STAY OFF TRESTLE. PENALTY FOR
TRESPASSING ON RAILROAD PROPERTY

And it was planted dead ahead of me, in the middle of my path as I continued to run alongside the train. I saw Lucky slip past it without even breaking her stride, but I would crash right into it, with nowhere else to go. Now I knew there was no other choice. I had to jump.

Then I heard a voice booming out behind me, over the noise of the train.

"GRAB ON T' ME!"

I risked a quick glance over my shoulder and saw Rafe,

the dining-car steward, crouching down on the steps of the diner, several cars behind the engine. One huge black arm was wrapped around the grab bar at the door, and his other was flung out, like the fireman reaching for train orders on a hoop. When the diner drew alongside me, I was running at about the same speed as the train. In that moment I reached for Rafe's neck, and he caught me around the waist and swept me up onto the diner. I saw the STAY OFF TRESTLE sign flash by us a second later. I staggered backward against the wall, gasping for breath.

"What you doin' out dere, chile? Don' you know takin' a walk on a railroad bridge is bad fo' yo' *health?*"

"I do *now!*" I panted. Then I saw Lucky. She was still running alongside the train and looking up into the doorway at us.

"Up, Lucky! JUMP!"

Rafe caught her by the collar, as her toenails clawed frantically at the metal steps, and pulled her into the car. "Dat dawg sho' kin run!" he said admiringly.

The engineer must have seen Rafe pull me onboard, because I felt the train accelerating now. And with two short blasts on the whistle: woop, woop, the "all clear" signal, we were soon barreling down the track.

Now that it was all over, with time to realize how close I had come to being killed, I began to tremble. Rafe took me into the galley and poured me a glass of water, then began to talk seriously.

"I bettuh go up and tell de hogger dat you onboard, safe an' all. And while I's gone, you don' go near dat door, y'hear me?"

A WW II troop sleeper

"Why? What's on the other side?"

"Why, honey-chile, you done landed on a *troop train!*"

So that's why I didn't know about a train along here now. Troop trains were unscheduled. "Is ... is that so bad?"

Rafe shook his big head sadly. "Dis train is full t' over-flowin' wid po' boys all shot up and wounded in de war ... some of 'em up here ..." He was tapping his forehead. "Don' know *what* dem po' boys is likely t' do, dey knows we got us a gal onboard de train. I jus' hope none of 'em seen you git on."

I hoped so, too! I was suddenly filled with despair. *Oh, why couldn't I stay out of trouble?* It's not as if I went looking for it! But trouble always seemed to be looking for *me!*

When Rafe came back from a conference with the engineer, he looked grave. And I imagined I knew why. It was my fault, for being in a place where I had no business being, and endangering myself and others, too. What if Rafe had lost his footing on those slick metal steps, while he hung out over the edge of the track to pull me onboard? We'd *both* have been killed! What if it had given the engineer a heart attack to see a kid running along the tracks in front of his train? And now he was mad at me.

To say nothing of what my father would be, by the time I got home! When *would* I get home? I wondered.

"Hogger say he don' stop dis train befo' Elko. Hand you over t' de man dere. Have 'em tell yo' daddy."

The dispatcher in Elko! My father's boss! And Elko was at least two hours away. I sat down at a table by the window and began to cry.

At first, my parents had not been worried about me. I often spent hours roaming around by myself, and my mother knew that I had packed a lunch and taken a canteen of water, too. And the dogs were with me.

But when Lucy came home by herself and first barked to come in the house and then barked to go right back out again, they began to worry. Daddy knew what direction I was headed, and when the section foreman came in a few minutes later in his little gasoline-powered car that ran on the tracks, my father asked him to go out again and take him along. When they came to the timber trestle and saw my bicycle leaning up against the berm, Daddy had an idea

A gasoline-powered track car

what had happened. He had seen the troop train when it stopped for coal and water in Shafter and now he started putting two and two together. He went back to the office and asked Jean to move over—he wanted to telegraph the other operators along the line, going toward Elko, and ask if anyone had heard or seen anything unusual. The operator at Wells answered that he had seen a girl in the diner of a troop train as it sped through his crossing. That, in itself, was something you didn't see every day! Then came the message from EJM (telegraphers always went by their initials), the dispatcher in Elko to GPS in Shafter: Daughter and dog arrived Elko, transferred to eastbound train No. 40.

He offered no further comment.

All the way back to Shafter on train No. 40, the exalted Exposition Flyer (the train I'd always wanted to ride), I thought about what I would say to my parents. One thing was certain. I had to tell them how Rafe had risked his own neck to save mine. That was sure to wipe his debt off Daddy's ledger—and *then* some!

When Lucky and I got off the train at Shafter, he was waiting for us on the platform. I hung my head, wondering what my punishment would be. My father had never laid a hand on me in anger, but I could tell by the grim look on his face that something along those lines might be in order now. Without a word, he led me into the depot where my mother, also tight-lipped and ashen, was waiting.

As anticipated, I started to get the lecture about how BIG and DANGEROUS a TRAIN can be, but I interrupted with a bold, "But, Daddy! It's not my fault! There's nothing to DO out here!"

My parents were silent, looking first at me and then at each other. After a long pause, my father said, "Well, Rosie, I guess we'd better get her a horse."

CHAPTER FIVE

Getting Dusty

A horse! *I was going to have my own horse!*

Daddy was laying out the plan. The "mustang man" was due along here any day now on his annual roundup (and, naturally, he owed my father money). He always stopped to buy supplies from Joe Thomas, whose store was the only one around for miles, and to have a friendly game of poker with my father, of course. This time, if the man had any attractive horses, why, he would propose a trade: a horse for what the man owed him, which was ten dollars.

I didn't want to think about what would happen to the rest of the horses the mustang man had captured, after we chose one of them. The poor things were *all* on their way to the glue factory at the moment, including mine. I knew horse traders couldn't feel sorry about that. They made their living by rounding up wild mustangs, out there on the desert in Utah and Nevada, on fast ponies of their own, specially trained to race alongside a quarry while the man swung a lasso and roped each one around the neck. Then they joined the others on their way to the slaughterhouse. *It made you sick just to think about it.*

While Daddy was talking, old Mr. McNight came into the office. The first time we met, Daddy told him jokingly that I was "the last Lady D'Anjou," whereupon the old gentleman had swept off his cap and bent at the waist in a low theatrical bow, murmuring, "An honor, your ladyship!"

He had a deep, resonant voice, and a manner of speaking that made you think you were watching a stage play. He could quote poetry by the hour, and long speeches by Shakespeare. I knew this because later on I started going over to his house, which was built of railroad ties, and listening to him. His looks were imposing, too. He was a husky man, despite his age (whatever it was), with a broad chest and strong shoulders under his black overalls and heavy cotton work shirt. His thick, pure white hair was partially hidden under a black cap, and while he was operating the coal chute, he wore a red bandanna tied over the lower part of his face, like a train robber in an old Western. When he pulled off the bandanna, as he did when he came into the office, it left him looking a little like a raccoon, with black rings around his eyes. But after he washed up, you could see that he had a handsome face, with crinkly brown eyes and a square jaw.

I was fascinated by old Mr. McNight—and so, I soon noticed, was my mother. She always smiled sweetly whenever she saw him, and she touched her hair in a way that made me suspicious. I had seen her flirtatious side once before, years ago in Sacramento, when she impulsively joined an Evangelical church, mostly because she was attracted to the minister, whose name was C. Mannly Ayers. My sister and I used to double up laughing while imitating him and his "manly airs." He had long bony fingers with polish on his nails and a way of talking that invited parody. The way he said "the Holy Speereet" cracked us up, which made my mother very cross.

She thought Mr. McNight was a "lovely old gentleman,"

which he was, but where he got a son like Orvy, I could never quite figure out. If old Mr. McNight sometimes looked like a raccoon, Orvy looked like a weasel. His mousy brown hair, which started low on his forehead, just above his beady eyes, grew straight back over his head, hiding his small ears, and his face seemed to come to a point in front, ending with a twitchy nose. He was crude. He had no manners. He left a trail of dirty coffee cups and cigar ashes on the counter whenever he came into the office.

My father was fastidious about himself and the telegraph office as well, so he didn't hesitate to tell Orvy (or anyone else) to clean up his mess. He often scolded Jean for leaving the office untidy at the end of her shift and the beginning of his. When Laura came on at midnight, she would always find the place immaculate.

In contrast to Orvy, no one had to tell old Mr. McNight to pick up after himself. He was addicted to Hershey bars and often came into the office eating one, but always put the wrapper in the wire wastebasket under the desk or jammed it back into the big front pocket of his overalls. He had no use for alcohol or tobacco, he used to say, but chocolate was something else again.

He was munching a candy bar now, as he listened to my father telling about arrangements we might make with the mustang trader.

"A horse! A horse! My kingdom for a horse!" cried old Mr. McNight. When we all turned and looked at him, he said, "Richard the Third."

He was like that.

I was much too excited to sleep that night, anticipating

the day the mustang trader would show up, so I was still awake when my father came home shortly after midnight, and I heard the discussion between my parents, in their room across the hall, about acquiring a horse. I was surprised that my mother had seemed to consent to the plan when it was first discussed earlier that day, and I was sure it would not be long before she would think better of the idea and be against it.

"Well, I'm against it," said my mother.

"But, Rosie," argued my father, "we promised her a horse and we can't go back on our word."

"*You* promised her a horse, I didn't."

"All right. But she hasn't got it yet, has she? And we don't know for sure if the mustang trader will even show up this year. Although . . ."

"Although what?"

"He always has."

"In addition to everything else, where are we going to keep this animal? I don't want him tramping around in my garden!"

"Well, you said yourself the soil could use some fertilizer."

"That's not the point. Where are we going to *keep* him?"

"In the corral adjacent to the railroad spur, I suppose. It's never used, except for cattle, and occasionally sheep, when they come through to be loaded into freight cars."

"And what if she gets hurt?"

"Don't worry, Mother. She knows how to ride."

"That's fine, but don't forget Blairsden!"

"What about Blairsden?"

"You don't remember the time she had to be rushed to

the hospital in Portola with a compound fracture, after that horse threw her off? What if she breaks her *neck* on this one?"

"That was a fluke. Anyway, you can't worry about her every time she—"

"What do you mean, 'a fluke?' How is this going to be any different?"

"Well, for one thing, in Blairsden she was riding bareback."

"You mean we have to buy a saddle, too?"

"I'm sure the mustang trader has an extra saddle he can let us have."

My mother went on grumbling until Daddy seemed to settle the argument by saying, "And besides, Rosie. These horses are wild—never been ridden before. It may take her months just to get a saddle on the beast. I doubt she'll ever really ride him. But in the meantime, it'll give her something to do."

(*And keep her away from trains, his tone seemed to suggest.*)

For the next few days I scanned the horizon first thing every morning and the last thing every night for some far-off sign of the mustangs. My father said I would see a cloud of dust before I could actually see any horses. While we waited, I was going to the corral next to the railroad spur every day and getting it ready to hold my horse. Daddy bought hay and feed from Joe Thomas, and I even borrowed a wheelbarrow and a shovel from him, so I could clean up after the last herd of cattle that had been in there. (Fertilizer for the garden, I told my mother, when I lugged it all back to the depot.)

I had to pass old Mr. McNight's house on my way to and from the corral. About the only thing that could distract me from my project was hearing his velvety voice reading poetry or reciting Shakespeare to an imaginary audience. His window was always open to let the smoke from his blackened cookstove escape, and sometimes I would linger for a few minutes and listen to him. Once, as I passed, I happened to glance up and catch sight of him pacing back and forth with something in his hand. I crept closer to the window and saw that it was a knife with a long, pointed blade. Then I heard his voice, booming out, "In Aleppo once, where a malignant and a turbaned Turk beat a Venetian and traduced the state, I took by the throat the circumcised dog and smote him *thus!*"

To my horror, I saw that he had raised the knife high above his head, and brought it down hard against his chest! I ran to the front door and pounded on it, screaming, "Mr. McNight! Mr. McNight! Open the door! . . . *Please!*"

The door opened quickly. "Why, Lady D'Anjou! Whatever is the matter?"

To my astonishment, there was no blood or any sign of a wound, and the "dagger" that he was still holding in his hand looked clean, too.

"Oh! . . . Are you all right? I . . . I'm sorry, but I saw you plunge that thing into your heart!" I said breathlessly.

"A harmless stage prop, my dear. Made of rubber. You see?" and he bent the blade double just to prove it.

I suddenly felt very foolish. "You were acting," I said. "I should have guessed."

"Othello, Act Five," he said. "But I'm pleased that you

found my performance convincing . . . Will you come in and have some tea?"

I did go in and have tea with him that day, and many days afterward. I often brought cookies with me, usually brownies, because I knew he loved chocolate. (And here, in lawless Nevada, you didn't have to worry about sugar rationing!)

Old Mr. McNight became my honorary grandfather. I'd never really known a grandfather. Daddy's father—the dashing Lord D'Anjou (alias George Smith)—had died shortly after I was born, and my mother's father had a heavy German accent and looked very severe when I didn't understand what he was saying, which was most of the time. But she used to tell me about *her* grandfather and show me his picture. He had been a cavalry officer in the Prussian army and looked very handsome in his uniform, with a long sword buckled across a white tunic with gold braid and spurs on his boots.

Old Mr. McNight made a perfect grandfather. He showed me his books, which took up most of the space in his little house, and got me interested in classical literature. Sometimes we would read together. And all the time I wondered how in the world he got to a place like Shafter, out here in the middle of nowhere, and how such a man could have produced a son like Orvy! Finally, one day, I asked, "How did you happen to come here, Mr. McNight? Why aren't you in the theater in some big city?"

He laughed and said, "Oh, I was, years ago. But I am like a poor player that struts and frets his hour upon the stage and then is heard no more . . . Macbeth, Act Five."

My mother's grandfather, a Prussian army officer

"So, you were on the stage? Where was that?"

"In England. I was 'born in a trunk,' as they say in the theater. My father was what is called an actor-manager and my mother was an actress in the same company. I went on the stage when I was just a boy. It's a hard life, you know."

I wanted to say, *"Harder than operating a coal chute?"* But I didn't.

"Eventually, we emigrated to Canada, my wife and I."

"Oh. Was Orvy's mother in the theater?"

After a pause he said, "In a kind of theater, yes."

"Did she do Shakespeare, too?"

"Oh, no. There was more of Lambeth Walk than Lady Macbeth in Abby," he chuckled.

"And what—"

He held up his hand. "Then must you speak of one who loved not wisely but too well."

"I know that one. It's Othello. Right after he kills Desdemona."

"Yes."

I had so many more questions: What happened to Abby? Did Orvy take after her? He certainly didn't take after his father. *Was* Mr. McNight Orvy's father? Did he kill Abby, like Othello killed Desdemona? (The rest of that speech goes, "of one not easily jealous, but, being wrought, perplexed in the extreme . . .") No, nothing in the world would convince me that gentle old Mr. McNight could kill anyone! His wife was gone, that much was certain, but he looked so sad that I decided not to ask any more questions. We never spoke of Abby again.

It seemed an eternity before I saw anything but little

"dust devils" churning up sand out in the desert, and nothing that looked like a cloud of dust made by a herd of mustangs. Then one day, there it was, moving toward us from the east.

"Daddy! Daddy! I think they're coming!"

I dragged him out to see, and sure enough, pretty soon we could make out a man on horseback leading a string of horses behind him. I ran to the corral and had to be restrained by my father from getting too close to the mustangs as they were herded into the enclosure. I was beside myself with joy.

There were a dozen or so horses in all, and two dogs constantly nipping at their heels. Mustangs are typically short, muscular horses that are said to be direct descendants of horses brought in by the Spaniards. They are hardy feral animals who live, and apparently thrive, in the harsh conditions of the western plains and deserts. The mustang man's herd seemed to come in several colors, ranging from a motley black/brown to a dusty white. It was the dusty white one that captured my attention right from the beginning. Most of them looked tired from their long journey, and just stood there regarding us passively, but the dusty white one raced around the corral and tossed his head, registering his objection to being confined. Once he kicked against the railing, setting the dogs to barking wildly.

After an exchange of greetings, my father began explaining his proposition to the horse trader.

"Think my daughter could eventually ride one of those mangy beasts?"

The man ran a hand over his stubbly chin before

A white mustang. *Courtesy Natalie Sachs, photographer*

answering. "Well, I dunno, George. They ain't broke to a saddle, y'know."

"No, I know that. She thinks she'd like to try and tame one, though. We'd take one of them off your hands for the ten spot you owe me. How does that sound?"

"Well, I dunno . . ."

"We need a saddle, too," I piped up. "And a bridle."

"All for ten dollars? You drive a hard bargain, Missy."

I pointed to their feet. "They're not shod," I said.

The mustang man laughed out loud at that. "Think I was going to put shoes on a bunch of critters that'll be dog food by next week?"

My father saw the expression on my face and said to the man, "I'd be obliged if you wouldn't mention that, Bill. She's an animal lover." Then, turning to me, he said, "Well, Punkin, which one do you think you want?"

Without a moment's hesitation, I pointed to the dusty white one and said, "I want him."

If my father was dismayed at seeing me pick the liveliest one of the bunch, he didn't show it. He was probably thinking about what he had said to my mother about my never being able to ride it anyway.

The man laughed again, and said, "Well, Missy, you ain't very observant, are ya? That 'him' is a 'her,' in case you ain't noticed!"

I blushed, but could not be dissuaded from my choice. "I'm going to call her Dusty," I said decisively.

"Well, Bill, I guess that's your answer. Now, what about my proposition?" He nodded toward the white horse still kicking up dust in the corral. "That horse and a saddle for the ten dollars you owe me."

"Don't carry extra saddles around with me, George, but I got one in my tack room back in Elko. I could mebbe put it on the train, have it here in a few days."

"What about a bridle?" I asked, eyeing the one with silver buckles on his own cayuse.

"Oh, well, now . . ."

"Tell you what, Bill. We'll have a little friendly game of

poker tonight at Joe Thomas's place, and settle the question of a bridle."

"And a halter," I said. "I'll need a rope halter, if she's never had a bit in her mouth."

The mustang man looked at me and then allowed as how he'd best get out of Shafter while he still had the shirt on his back!

That night the men all played poker at the General Store and Post Office, and the next day I had a horse named Dusty, a bridle (with silver buckles), a rope halter, and a saddle to be shipped to us by train in a few days. I was in heaven—though I cried when I saw the mustang trader leaving with the rest of his horses, now all destined to become dog food in a week.

Being young and full of optimism, I naturally brushed aside all warnings of what I might be up against, trying to break a wild mustang and turn him (or rather, *her*) into a saddle horse. And if I had expected to get up and ride as soon as the saddle arrived from Elko, I was sadly mistaken.

Dusty had seen the other horses leaving, too, and had dashed around the corral, whinnying loudly after them. I sat on the top rail of the gate and tried to tell her how lucky she was that she wasn't going with them on the last leg of their trek to the slaughterhouse.

Every morning after walking down the line of boxcars on the Nevada Northern tracks with my mother, and then going on to little Nita's house for her English lesson, I raced back to the corral to fork hay over the fence and fill the trough with fresh water.

"Don't try to get into the corral with her," my father warned, "Let her come to you."

Yes, Daddy, but horses aren't fish. What am I supposed to use for bait?

And then I had an idea. The next morning I walked out to the corral with an apple in my pocket. I climbed up on the top rail as usual and sat there munching on the apple. Dusty was watching me with interest, so I held out my hand and said, "You want this?" She took a few steps toward me, then backed away, so I took another bite. She turned her head to one side and fixed me in a steady gaze from one big brown eye, as if to say, "What do I have to do to get it?" But it wasn't long before she came a little closer and stretched her neck out toward my hand. I said, "You're going to have to take it. I'm not going to drop it on the ground." She shook her head all around, but didn't back away. *If she bites my hand off, I'm really going to be in trouble!* But when she took the apple in her mouth, it only tickled the palm of my open hand.

Every morning after that, when I left the depot, I carried an apple for Dusty. (I told my mother they were for me, after she said she hoped I was not wasting them on that horse!) I soon found that if I held an apple in one hand and the halter in the other, Dusty would not shy away. The next thing was to put the halter around her neck, which was more difficult, but eventually she let me do it. Cautiously, I slid down off the railing and stood beside her, holding the rope. She bolted, and I had to let go of the rope, but stood my ground as she raced around the corral. In a few days I was able to lead her around by the halter.

Now for the saddle.

Laura sometimes came out to watch my progress with Dusty. She was an experienced rider, herself, but said she wouldn't be caught dead trying to ride a wild mustang! The saddle that the trader had shipped from Elko was a nice one—Daddy must have upped the ante in that poker game—in tooled leather with bright silver studs. I bought a can of saddle soap at the General Store and shined it up, "purty enough for the rodeo," as Laura said.

There was a little shed next to the corral where I kept the saddle, along with the feed and a currycomb for grooming. Every morning I took the saddle out of the shed and hoisted it up to the top rail. I sat in it a couple of times to adjust the stirrups, while Dusty watched me cautiously. *Now, people say that horses are stupid, but if you weighed half a ton and had a brain the size of a walnut, you'd be stupid, too!* They may not be able to sit down and figure things out on paper, like an Einstein or a Galileo, but what they lack in brain size, they make up in what we call "horse sense." Dusty knew exactly what that saddle was for and might even have recalled the mustang man sitting in one just like it. I could see her making up her mind right then and there: all the apples in the store were not going to make her hold still for *that!*

I had heard that it was possible to lead a horse out of a burning barn by putting a sack over his head, so he can't see what he's afraid of. I found a clean feed sack and slipped it over Dusty's head, while I led her around the corral a few times. When I reached the place where I had left the saddle, I tied the end of the halter to the fence, then carefully lifted the saddle off the rail and slid it onto her back. At first she threw her head around to the side and tried to get hold of it with her teeth, but she couldn't bite through the feed sack. Slowly, I untied the rope and began leading her around the corral again. So far, so good. The next step would be reaching under her belly to cinch it up, loosely at first, and then a little tighter when she was more used to it. After that, I would be able to take the sack off her head.

The first time I tried to get into the saddle, while I had her tied to the fence, Dusty put her ears back and bit me, tearing a hole in my shirt and leaving an ugly red and purple bruise on my side. I would have to hide the shirt from my mother when I got home. It was the first of several pieces of clothing to be kept out of sight, under my bed. (Luckily, my mother was a terrible housekeeper and never swept under there.)

"Daddy, can you get rabies from a horse bite?"

"I don't think so, honey. Why? Did Dusty bite you?"

"Oh, no. I was just wondering."

I soon found that sliding into the saddle from the height of the top rail in the fence was easier (and safer) than trying to get my foot in the stirrup before Dusty took a bite out of me. This had to be done very carefully, of course, and several times I found myself on the ground before I knew it. Other times she would trot around the corral, trying to scrape me off by rubbing against the fence, until I learned to throw my leg over the saddle horn, out of the way. Before that, the outside seam of two pairs of pants got shredded by the rough wood of the rails and had to be hidden under my bed.

So far, I was still using the halter. The bridle would come

next, but getting the bit in her mouth was going to be tricky. An apple again proved to be the answer.

I would hold the apple in my left hand and the bridle (behind my back) with my right. Then, when she reached for the apple, I would put the bit in her mouth and slip the straps over her ears, fastening the silver buckles while she munched the apple. That was the plan, anyway, and eventually it worked, but it took time. Once she was used to the bridle, I could lead her around the corral, holding onto the reins. Occasionally she would bump me playfully on the arm with her nose, as if to say, "I'm bored with this game. Let's do something more exciting." I didn't mind the bumping, but when she folded her ears back against her head, that's when you had to watch out! Next I tried sitting in the saddle and teaching her what the reins meant when they were laid across her neck, to the left or to the right.

Laura was impressed. She was leaning against the corral, watching us go from a trot to an easy gallop. Dusty was straining at the reins a little more on each lap. On about the third time around the enclosure, I said, "Open the gate!"

"Aw, now, Slim . . . I don't think—"

"Open the gate, Laura! She's about the jump the fence!"

The gate swung open and we shot through it, leaving Laura in a cloud of dust and sand. Pulling on the reins had no effect, so I just let the horse go, hell-bent-for-leather, and tried to stay on. She ran for miles in a straight line, and I was beginning to wonder how I was going to get *off*, when the problem solved itself, sooner than expected. She had spotted a patch of green grass growing around an old abandoned well, and she stopped so abruptly that I went right over her neck and landed on the ground with a thud. It made me see stars for a minute, just like the ones my mother had painted on the ceiling in my bedroom! But afterward I was able to pick myself up and determine that I had no broken bones. I walked over to Dusty, who was calmly eating the grass, and picked up the reins.

"Well, old girl, I think we ought to enter you in the Derby!" All the horses I had ridden before were tired old nags, compared to this one.

The next question was how to persuade this maverick to turn around and head home again. I slipped the reins over her neck and swung myself up into the saddle. When she had finished eating (and not before) I was able to turn her around. We headed back—but this time at a slower pace.

Laura was still waiting anxiously by the corral, though we had been gone the better part of an hour. She had been on the point of asking Joe Thomas, who owned a kind of jeep vehicle that he used for hunting, to organize a search party when she saw us cantering along in the distance.

After weeks of enduring sore, aching muscles, bites, bruises, and even a sprained wrist, I had accomplished what I set out to do. My father, noting my injuries, said he didn't know which of us—me or the horse—would be "broken" first! Through it all my mother shook her head and wrung her hands, but had to concede that Daddy's idea of acquiring a horse, for the purpose of giving me something to do, was working. I was staying off of (and out from under) trains.

"Mommy, Laura's going to a movie tonight in Wendover. Can I go with her?"

"*May* I go with her," my mother corrected me.

"All right, *may* I go?"

"When would you get back?"

"She's going up on No. 40 and coming back on a 'milk run' at 10:00, so she can be here in time to go to work at midnight."

My mother voiced her usual concerns about my staying up so late, and whether it would be an appropriate movie for children, but finally consented. So, Laura, in her best pair of Levi's and cowboy boots, and I in a similar pair of Levi's that I had bought (over my mother's objections) on our latest shopping trip to Elko, boarded Train No. 40, the Exposition Flyer, at 4:00 that afternoon. We were on our way to a night out in a "big" town.

It would be the longest night in my young life.

The place where we were going was, in fact, *two* towns. Wendover, Nevada, was first along the Western Pacific line, and next came Wendover, Utah, just across the border. There were even two train stations, only blocks apart. The State Line Hotel, a wide-open gambling, dining, and drinking establishment, as well as a hotel, straddled the border. The only movie theater was in the larger of the two, in Wendover, Utah.

I have no memory of the movie we saw that night, because of what happened afterward.

It was a long picture and we had to run to the train station in time to catch the "milk run." Rounding the end of the depot, Laura hissed, "Shee-oot!"

"What? What's the matter?"

"The clock in the movie house must've been slow . . . There goes our train."

She was right. With a sinking feeling, I watched the

retreating red lights on the last car disappearing down the track. "What about a later one?" Even as I said it, I knew the answer. There were no other passenger trains that night. But how about a freight?

Laura's Texas accent always got stronger when she was agitated. "Eight o'clock t'morrow mornin'—and yore Daddy shore ain't gonna be pleased!"

Not to mention what my *mother* would say! We could get the dispatcher there to wire Daddy that I was spending the night in Wendover, but Laura's situation was more serious. She had to relieve him at midnight in the office. If she wasn't there, he and Jean would have to split Laura's shift and they would both be cross—especially Jean, who didn't trust "that redhead." (Never mind that she was a redhead, too.) Jean had never liked her since Laura had belted her husband, Orvy, for getting fresh.

Laura was pointing off into the dark. "Wait a minute! . . . What's that over there?"

"Where?"

"Over yonder on the far track . . . C'mon, Slim!"

I saw Laura take off across the tracks, heading for a passenger train on the other side. "Wait! Where's it *going?*"

"Who cares? The engine's smokin' and it's pointin' in the right direction! C'mon!"

I ran after her and we jumped into the first vestibule between cars that we came to. The train wasn't moving yet, so we seemed to have plenty of time to go into the next car and take a seat. I knew we could "pull the ripcord" and stop the train when we got close to Shafter, although engineers didn't like you to do that.

Laura pushed open the door, with me close behind her. What we saw then made my blood run cold.

Every conceivable space was occupied by men sitting or half-lying on seats, and even spilling out into the aisle. Inside that car I saw more uniforms, crutches, and bandages than I had seen in newsreels of men returning from the battlefront. Some had their heads bandaged, others their arms in slings; some had legs in casts, stuck out into the aisle for more room. The worst thing was the desolation on their faces. I wanted to cry, but I was too scared.

Rafe's words came back to me, "You done landed on a *troop train!* It's full t' overflowin' wid po' boys all shot up and wounded in de war. No tellin' what dem po' boys do, dey knows we got us a gal onboard."

I grabbed hold of Laura's hand and tugged at it. Half over her shoulder she said, "Stand your ground."

I wanted to say, "Laura! This isn't the Alamo! Let's get *out* of here!" But when I opened my mouth, nothing came out. I couldn't believe what she did next. She started walking slowly *forward* and pulling me along with her.

"We're gonna walk through t' the other end. The train's not movin' yet. We still got a chance to jump off when we get to the vestibule."

If we get to the vestibule! But I understood the risk she was prepared to take. To turn and run at that point might have caused a riot. Throughout the car there was total silence, with faces all turned toward us now. Some looked hostile, some blank, some curious.

After what seemed like an eternity, we reached the middle of the car. But our progress at that point was stopped by a soldier who stood up, right in front of Laura, and blocked the way. I could feel my heart beating wildly inside my chest, but Laura just stood there calmly, without saying a word.

After staring each other down for another minute, the soldier said, "You don't play poker, do you?"

Laura put one hand on her hip (the one that wasn't still gripping mine) and said, "Where I come from, ya *smile* when ya say that, pard-ner." And I thought: She really *is* a "tough Texas lady, scared o' nuthin'," after all!

I peeked around Laura and saw that the soldier standing in front of her was smiling! Then a voice across the aisle said, "Hey, Red! You from Texas?"

"Big D!" said Laura proudly.

"Jim, here, is from Fort Worth!"

"Howdy, neighbor," said Laura, and reached out to shake the boy's hand, but the one he put out in return was his left. I gasped as I saw that his right sleeve was empty, but Laura never flinched. Instead, she shook the hand that was offered, and even said admiringly, "You got quite a grip there, soldier."

"So do you, ma'am," he said.

Then, without missing a beat she said, "Well, boys, how 'bout that game? We gonna play poker, or not?"

"What about her?" asked the man who was blocking our way. "She play, too?"

"Why, Slim, here, is the best dang poker player in the sorry state of Nevada!"

"Except for my daddy," I squeaked.

"Yeah, except for her daddy," Laura conceded.

A deck of cards came out, suitcases and duffle bags were stood on end in the aisle to sit on, and a metal footlocker was set in the middle as a makeshift table.

Laura was shuffling the cards when another voice was heard. "Did you say Nevada? Is that where we are?" The boy's eyes were completely covered in white bandages.

"Wish I could tell ya different," said Laura. "Where y'all from?"

A chorus of voices answered, "Oklahoma," "Illinois," "New York," "Minnesota," and almost every other state in the Union.

"What do you do out here?" asked the boy whose eyes were bandaged.

"Work for the railroad."

"Doin' what?"

"Telegrapher," said Laura.

"I'm in the Signal Corps. You understand this?" and he took out a heavy black fountain pen and began tapping out a message on the metal footlocker.

I blushed and Laura grinned. "Slim knows Morse Code, too, so keep it clean, son!"

There was a general round of laughter and applause. I began to relax. *All the same, I wished the train would start!*

Laura won the first two poker hands and I won the third. Finally, with a lurch, the train began to move. We were on our way home.

Laura stood up and pulled "the ripcord" when we heard the engineer blowing for the crossing at Shafter.

"Well, boys, hate to leave y'all, but this is where me and Slim get off."

As we walked through the car, there were whistles and cheers and a chorus of "Take it easy, Red!" and "So long, Slim!" A minute later we were standing on the platform at Shafter, waving and smiling as the train rolled past, and on down the tracks. I turned to look at Laura and was surprised to see that her face was wet with tears. That tough Texas lady was scared o' nuthin', all right—*except seeing her husband, Johnny, come home like the boys on that train.*

CHAPTER SIX

Celebrating V-J Day

It was the middle of August now, and the prospect of having to start school in that one-room schoolhouse, early next month, loomed larger and more depressing with each passing day. I rode Dusty, instead of my bicycle, as much as I could now (steering clear of any old abandoned wells with grass growing around them), and Lucky and Lucy "came along for the ride." But not poor old Moocher, who considered racing around after a horse just too much effort.

I was in the office one afternoon when Daddy took off his earphones and said he needed to go "out back." I had a suspicion that he was keeping a bottle of whiskey in the outhouse marked "Men," behind the baggage room. (It was the one place he could be sure that my mother wouldn't find it.) And each time he came in from a trip "out back" his eyes always looked a little brighter. It worried me that he was drinking on the job. He had been warned about it once already. *That snitch, Jean McNight, had reported him to the dispatcher in Elko.*

The telegraph terminal began clicking. I picked up the earphones so I could hear more clearly what was coming over the wire. No trains were due, so I knew it was not a set of orders to be copied and handed up to the trainmen.

But what I heard made my heart beat wildly.

When my father came back, I cried excitedly, "Daddy! Listen to this! It's about the WAR!"

We stood there listening together, and then he ran to the door of the agent's quarters, and called, "Rosie! What do you *think?* The WAR is over!"

My mother, with relief evident on her face, rushed into the office, still wearing her painting smock.

Although May 8, called V-E Day—for Victory in Europe—was officially the end of World War II, the Japanese had not yet surrendered three months later. Fierce battles raged in the Pacific, with terrible American casualties. President Truman had issued a warning to the Japanese in July, during an international conference in some place called Potsdam, to surrender or suffer "prompt and utter destruction." The Japanese had ignored the warning.

So, why had they surrendered now? There was no more information coming over the wire. My father said we should go and see if there was anything more about it on Joe Thomas's radio, so the three of us trooped across the tracks to the General Store and Post Office.

What we heard over the radio shocked us. The president had unleashed a devastating new weapon, called an atomic bomb, against Japan. Last week one had been dropped on Hiroshima, and three days later another one on Nagasaki. Upwards of 100,000 had been killed in both cities. Many more who had survived the blasts, but were horribly burned by something called "radiation," would surely die, too. We heard that America was now celebrating today, August 14, as V-J Day—for Victory over Japan. People all across the country were dancing in the streets! Perfect strangers were kissing each other in Times Square!

I sat stunned in Joe Thomas's living room, after hearing

the radio broadcast. Yes, I had wanted the new president to end this awful war, but not by annihilating hundreds of thousands of Japanese citizens! I thought of all the Japanese people, back in California, who had been treated so badly by our government—sent away to "relocation camps," which were little better than prisons—not for anything they did, but simply because they were Japanese. (And my mother had worried that we might suffer the same fate, simply because we were German.) I had to believe that people in Japan—just ordinary people, like us—didn't like this war any better than we did. It was their leaders who were wrong, in the same way *our* leaders were sometimes wrong. And now the people, not their leaders, were paying the price. President Truman said he had ordered the bombs dropped on Japanese cities in order to save thousands of American servicemen's lives.

I didn't envy him. Presidents have to make a lot of hard choices.

I could see that no one else in Joe Thomas's living room thought the same way I did. Daddy and Joe were shaking hands and clapping each other jovially on the shoulder. (*Even that old sourpuss, Grace Thomas, was grinning from ear to ear.*)

It was only a little after 4:00 p.m. and my father had just started his shift in the office, but he said that we ought to celebrate by going into Wendover for dinner and a "good time." My mother seemed apprehensive about the "good time" part of it, and with good reason. She knew it would mean drinking, probably lots of it. But Daddy was in such good humor that she finally consented to going in and changing out of her painting smock while I ran over to Laura's house to ask if she would take the first four or five hours of my father's shift for him. He would make it up to her the next day, he said.

We were just in time to board the eastbound Flyer, which usually did not stop in Shafter, but could be flagged down for passengers. Daddy had put on a proper jacket, over his black trousers, and my mother had put on a nice dress. She made me put on a skirt, too. Now, standing on the platform, we had the appearance of a well-dressed family setting off for dinner and a "good time" in Wendover.

Concealed under his jacket, I knew, was my father's silver hip flask, which he carried "for emergencies," he always said with a wink. Today's "emergency" was a trip on the train into Wendover, forty miles away.

He'd had the polished silver flask all through Prohibition and the Great Depression, because, as he said, in those dark days when you most needed a drink, you couldn't buy one. The flask was about eight inches tall, slim and slightly concave, to fit snugly into a gentleman's hip pocket. My father used to say that whenever you met one of your good friends on the street you would always ask him if he had "anything on his hip."

By the time the train arrived in Wendover, Daddy had been to the men's toilet twice, and his eyes had become very bright. I was bracing for trouble.

The State Line Hotel, as I mentioned, straddled the border between Utah and Nevada in the twin towns of Wendover. We got off the train at the first station, Wendover, Nevada, and walked the block or so to the hotel. The streets were crowded with people celebrating V-J Day in the same ways that people all over the country were celebrating—

only in this wide-open section of the Wild West, in addition to people shouting and cars honking, there was also the sound of Rebel yells as men on horseback raced through the streets, firing guns into the air. My mother and I clung together and walked close to Daddy.

Just outside the bar, adjacent to the dining room and hotel entrance to the State Line, Daddy stopped and suggested we go in to "wet our whistles" before dinner. (The sign on the door advertised "Tables for Ladies.") My mother said she preferred to have dinner and then catch an early train back to Shafter. But the noise on the sidewalk was deafening and she wanted to get off the street, so she agreed to go in and have something nonalcoholic.

Daddy was pushing open the swinging door when he spotted Rafe (it was hard to miss a man of his size) coming along the sidewalk and greeted him with a big bear hug.

"Rosie! Look who's here! This is the man we have to thank for saving our little girl's *life.*"

The look on my mother's face said she wondered what kind of nonsense he was talking *this* time, so I stood close to her ear and explained that it was Rafe, the man on the troop train who had pulled me up into the diner, and off the railroad trestle, just in time.

"Meet the Zulu!" said my father, expansively, but there was so much noise in the street that my mother thought he said "Missoula," and assumed the man was from Montana. So she said stiffly, "How do you do, Missoula?"

Daddy doubled up laughing at that. Then, clapping Rafe on the shoulder, he said, "Come on in and have a drink! M' wife won't drink with me, and Evelyn's underage, so you'll have to keep me company. A man can't drink alone, y' know!" (*Although he did it all the time.*)

"Now, Mistuh Smith," Rafe scolded gently, "You knows I don' drink!"

"Aw, we're just going to wet our whistles, then go in for dinner. Come on, now." And he pushed open the door. Rafe allowed himself to be pulled along by the arm into the bar. My mother and I followed, both of us now very apprehensive.

At one of the "tables for ladies," Daddy sat us all down and said, "What'll you have?" My mother asked for a root beer and I said, "Me, too." Rafe said he would have the same. My father then stepped over to the bar, built of sturdy dark wood with a brass rail at the bottom, which ran the length of the room. Slapping one hand down on the bar, he shouted, "Barkeep!"

The bartender, obviously no stranger to my father, came over and said, "Why, hullo there, Mr. Smith. Ain't seen you in here for a while. What'll it be?"

"The usual for me, son, and my companions all want root bear. Including the Zulu!" and he laughed loudly.

Now the bartender was looking apprehensive, too, and I wondered why, so I left my mother and Rafe sitting at the table and went "to help Daddy," I said.

I walked over and stood next to my father. The bartender was saying in a low, uneasy tone, "It ain't *me,* Mr. Smith. You know that. But there's an ugly bunch of coyotes down there, at the far end, and they ain't lookin' too happy just at the moment." He jerked his head toward five or six men hunkered over the bar, in chaps and cowboy boots, their Stetsons tipped far back on their heads. All eyes were turned our way.

"Hmph!" snorted my father. And then, dismissing them as "Saddle tramps . . . drifters," he paid the bartender and picked up two of the drinks that had been poured for us—his large whiskey and one of the root beers. I picked up the other two and followed him to the table. "Here we are, folks!" he said genially.

He was still holding the two glasses when a voice behind him said, "Hold on there." I froze when I saw that one of the saddle tramps, with a gun jammed into his belt, was standing right behind Daddy. I looked back at the other men and noticed a rifle leaning against the bar next to one of them. "We don't drink with no Zulus!"

My father said calmly, still holding the two glasses in his hand, "Well, then, I guess you better do your drinkin' some-place *else*, cowboy!"

"I got no quarrel with you, Pops," began the drifter, "but we just won the war, in case you ain't heard." He was looking directly at Rafe now, and Rafe was looking directly back at him—with a kind of smile on his face! "Y'see, boy, we're all 'mericans in here, so you kin just take your black butt—"

The man never had a chance to finish that sentence. My father, still with his back to him, was setting the glasses down on the table, and I noticed that his hands were coming up in fists as he did so. When he turned around, he threw a one-two combination punch that would have dropped the legendary Jack Johnson if he wasn't looking for it! With a loud groan, the cowboy stumbled backward, hit his head on the brass rail of the bar as he went down, and lay still.

"*George!*" screamed my mother, and her hands flew up to her face. There was a look of terror in her eyes.

I wasn't feeling so good, either, but I wasn't sorry for what my father had done. The guy had it coming!

Now, however, there was hell to pay. The rest of the "ugly bunch of coyotes" was pounding down the wooden floor, spurs jangling. One of them grabbed my father around the neck and another hit him in the stomach. In the next second, Rafe was on his feet and pulling the men off, dragging one in each huge hand toward the door. He threw them both out onto the sidewalk and then turned back to the table, but two more were waiting for him. Now the whole room seemed to erupt in one wild brawl. *Just like in the old Westerns.*

In the confusion, I wasn't sure what happened next, but Daddy and Rafe both had their hands full, fighting off attackers. Daddy went down and lay unconscious on the floor. Out of the corner of my eye I saw the one remaining cowboy at the end of the bar pick up the rifle that had been leaning against it and start toward us. When he got to where my father was lying, he bent over him with the rifle butt aimed at his head. Before I knew what I was doing, I picked up a heavy wooden chair and brought it down as hard as I could over the man's head. With a loud, splintering sound— whether from the chair breaking or the man's skull, I wasn't sure—he fell over. The rifle clattered harmlessly to the floor beside him.

The room was now in total chaos, with men throwing punches and bottles and chairs all around us. I grabbed my mother, now almost paralyzed with fear, and shouted,

"Mommy! Help me get Daddy up. We've got to get out of here!"

My father was coming around now, although he was still somewhat punch-drunk, and between my mother and me, we managed to get him up on his feet and steer him toward the door. Out on the sidewalk, people were crowding around, trying to get a look at the barroom brawl still going on inside. With Daddy leaning heavily on both our shoulders, we began walking toward the train station. Then I saw the blood gushing from an ugly gash over his eye, and said, "Wait. Let's get him over to the hospital and have that sewn up." I knew the Western Pacific maintained a small hospital-clinic in Wendover for its employees in the area.

My mother was not at all happy about taking Daddy to a doctor—being, at least for the moment, still a Christian Scientist, and angry enough to let him bleed to death, besides! But she grudgingly conceded that it was probably the right thing to do, so we headed off in the direction of the hospital, with Daddy now fully awake and asking for his silver hip flask.

At the hospital, we had to wait for more than an hour while a weary doctor patched up other casualties from the V-J Day celebrations. Eventually, however, the cut over my father's eye was sewn up, and the bleeding stopped. (The pain had been eased by some pills the doctor gave him, washed down with the last of the whiskey from the hip flask.) Soon the Smith family, all of us a little the worse for our "good time" in Wendover, boarded the last "milk run" back to Shafter.

Laura had worked most of Daddy's shift already, but

when we got off the train she saw that he was in no condi-
tion to relieve her. My mother and I took him into the
agent's quarters and put him to bed at the end of a long—
and memorable—V-J Day, 1945.

The next morning Daddy was up at 6:00 and going to
the office, saying he felt "fit as a fiddle," despite the big white
bandage plastered over the cut above his eye. In the office
he even joked with Laura about the previous night's adventures in Wendover, declaring that he'd never enjoyed himself
more—though of course he couldn't remember "all the
details."

But that was my father. He genuinely *liked* to drink, and
willingly suffered the consequences, always insisting that
he'd had a fine time. Never mind that it was jeopardizing his
job, his marriage, and his health. (Years later, on his deathbed,
he would laugh and say, "But look at all the fun I've had!")

I got up early too, but I wasn't feeling "fit as a fiddle." I
was worried about what might have happened to Rafe,
who was nowhere to be seen by the time my mother and
I managed to get Daddy out of the saloon. I was sorry about
leaving Rafe alone, to carry on the fight that my father had
started, but it seemed the only thing to do. We had to be
gone when the "ugly coyote" that I had bashed over the
head with a chair woke up. The sight of the man lying on
the floor with the rifle still close by his side gave me night-
mares, once I was finally able to get to sleep!

When I wandered into the office later in the morning,
I noticed that Daddy's mood had changed. He was sitting
in his chair, staring into space, and hardly seemed to notice
when I spoke to him.

"What's wrong, Daddy?"

It turned out that Laura had received a message late last night from the dispatcher in Wendover, saying that a Western Pacific employee had been arrested on a charge of inciting a riot and been fined $500, which he was unable to pay, so the judge had ordered him held in jail.

"Rafe?"

My father nodded. I think he was just then beginning to remember some of the "details" of the previous night.

"What are we going to do?"

Looking up at me with a blank expression, he said, "Who?"

"Well, Daddy, if anybody 'incited a riot' in Wendover last night, it was *you*, not Rafe!"

When my mother came into the office I told her about Rafe. "Five hundred dollars!" she gasped. "Does he have that kind of money?"

My father shook his head. "No, of course not."

"Does that mean he'll have to stay in jail?"

"Until he can pay the fine. That's what the judge said."

Then he swung his chair around, unlocked his "bug," and began sending out messages over the wire to everyone who owed him money, starting with the ones most able to pay, the other agents up and down the line. He was calling in his "markers," or IOUs, not for himself—he would never do that—but for Rafe.

I was proud of him.

While the three of us waited for answers to Daddy's wires, I felt obliged to confess that I had twenty-five dollars, and I wanted to help pay Rafe's fine.

My mother stared at me. "Twenty-five dollars! Where did you get it?"

Now my secret would have to come out. "I won it," I said, and waited for the axe to fall.

"Won it?" said my parents in a single voice.

"Uh-huh."

"How?" asked my father.

"Playing pool."

Now my mother starting echoing everything I said, but shouting it. "YOU WON IT PLAYING POOL!"

"Yes."

"Who did you play with?" asked my father.

"The Mexican section men."

"THE MEXICAN SECTION MEN!" shouted my mother.

"When?" asked my father.

"Usually on Friday afternoons. That's their payday."

"YOU PLAYED POOL WITH MEXICANS ON PAYDAYS!" shouted my mother.

"Yes."

"This is all your fault, George!"

"*My* fault! How do you figure that? I didn't teach her to play pool!"

"You taught her to *gamble!*"

"I taught her to play cards, not to gamble. Poker is a gentleman's game. Pool is for bums."

"Oh, no, Daddy! Pool takes skill, just like poker!"

"WELL," shouted my mother, "THERE'LL BE NO MORE OF EITHER ONE FOR YOU, YOUNG LADY!"

"She made a good point, though, Mother. If she wants to donate her twenty-five dollars to a good cause, we'll let her." And turning to me, he said, "Go get your money, sweetheart."

All that day, answers came flooding in from people who owed my father money. At 4:30 in the afternoon he took the Flyer into Wendover and paid Rafe's fine. My mother insisted that I go along with him to make sure he didn't stop at the State Line Hotel to "wet his whistle."

CHAPTER SEVEN

Reading, Writing, 'Rithmetic

As the fateful day approached when I would finally have to start school, my arguments with my mother grew more frequent and heated. (My father tried to stay out of it.) She often assumed her most-menacing Prussian hausfrau stance—feet apart and planted firmly under her, hands on hips—to say, "Now, see here! You can still learn something in that school! Don't think you can't!"

And I would often shout my last rude words on the subject and then run out of the room in tears.

I had met "horrible old Mrs. Hoppe," as I called her, one day in the office when she came in to pick up a Railway Express package. I had already made up my mind to hate her, and so of course I did. The first thing about her that annoyed me was the little nervous laugh she gave for no reason at all. It was like a wheeze, followed by a snort. When Daddy introduced us, she said, "Well, well. So you're going to be in my school, are you?" (Wheeze, snort.)

She was more or less as Daddy had described her ("blind as a bat and twice as ugly!") but, to be absolutely fair to the poor woman, it wasn't so much that she was *ugly*, as that she was just fat and dumpy in her dowdy, shapeless dresses. Her hair was a sort of drab "dishwater blonde," cropped off short just below the ears, and kinked up by what might have been a bad home permanent. The skin on her face was sallow and leathery, but it was her eyes that held your interest. You couldn't even tell what color they were. They were never more than slits, being screwed up in a constant squint. And she wasn't exactly *blind,* either, just terribly near-sighted. As Daddy had said, she could see well enough if something was literally "right under her nose," or almost *touching it.* I had the feeling that if she had worn glasses they would have been as thick as Coke bottle bottoms. And I wondered why she *didn't* wear glasses. It couldn't have been vanity. Not unless she was deluding herself about her looks! (There was that old saying: "Men never make passes at girls who wear glasses.") But Mrs. Hoppe was no girl, that much was certain, though it was difficult to say just how old she actually was. My father's guess was that she would "never see forty-five again." Anyway, she didn't need men making passes at her because she already had a husband, which was hard to believe, too. But then, he was no prize, either.

Like "The Old Woman Who Lived in a Shoe," Mrs. Hoppe lived in nearly as unlikely a place. She and Mr. Hoppe, along with their two little girls, occupied the old yellow ochre boxcar that my father had told me the Western Pacific was good enough to donate, and he and some of the other men had fitted out with windows and a proper door. Daddy sent me over there one day with a message about another package the lady was expecting via Railway Express. Her "house" wasn't hard to find. The heavy crane that brought it to its present site had lifted it off its steel wheels and set it down on concrete blocks. A paint job of sorts couldn't hide the fragmented Western Pacific logo, still partially visible between the door and windows. Toward one end, a black metal chimney poked through the roof, evidence of some kind of stove for heating and cooking within its drafty walls. (Boxcars have little or no insulation.)

Mr. Hoppe answered my knock. In contrast to Mrs. Hoppe, he was as thin as a rail. (Like Jack Spratt and his wife.) The expression on his stubbly face (didn't anyone in this God-forsaken place ever *shave?*) was more bewilderment than anything else. His brown/gray hair was thin and wispy and covered only part of his small head. He was wearing heavy brown cotton pants that were too long and too big around for him, so they were rolled up at the bottom and cinched in at the waist with a limp leather belt. His shirt looked like the "before" picture in an ad for Rinso laundry soap, promising "a cleaner, whiter wash." As far as anyone knew, Mr. Hoppe did not work, but instead was a kind of "househusband." The family apparently lived solely on Mrs. Hoppe's salary as a schoolmarm.

He explained that his wife was "out back," which could either mean that she was hanging clothes on the line or that she was in the outhouse. (I didn't ask which, although I did spot a galvanized metal tub and scrub board sitting on a washstand in what passed for a kitchen.) The clamor going on behind his back, as Mr. Hoppe stood at the door talking to me, was a loud and boisterous fight between his children that he was trying hard to ignore.

The girls, Violet and Dorothy, were rolling around on the bare floor of their boxcar home, pulling each other's hair and screaming. One was a little bigger than the other, but as Mr. Hoppe explained over the ruckus, the bigger one (Violet) was younger, at just six years old, and the smaller one (Dorothy) was older, aged seven. I looked past them at what more I could see of the interior of the boxcar. If I had ever considered the agent's quarters in the depot to be the nadir of gracious living, I would have to revise my opinion now. I would never want to trade places with this family of four crowded, as they were, into a ten-foot by forty-foot space, with sheets hung from the ceiling to divide it into "rooms." In the Hoppe household, moreover, there was not even a cold water tap in the "kitchen," which meant that all water had to come from a well outside, brought in and heated on the stove for baths and washing clothes. Still, I marveled that neither Mr. Hoppe nor the girls seemed to lack basic cleanliness. Nor had Mrs. Hoppe when I had seen her in the office.

The whole scene was too depressing. I gave my father's message about the Railway Express package to Mr. Hoppe and quickly left.

In contrast to the schoolmarm's boxcar, the place where Laura lived was the best house in the tiny community. As I mentioned, it was built of real wood and not smelly, creosote-soaked railroad ties like the rest of them. The depot was also built of real wood, and so was the General Store and Post Office, but these were the only ones, as far as I could tell.

I spent as much time with Laura as possible now, because soon I would be cooped up in that dungeon of a school-house most of the day. We still "hopped a freight" now and then (to my mother's annoyance) and rode out in the engine or the caboose of one train, and back again on another. We always tried to get on a train where our favorite conductor, Mr. Parker, was in charge of the caboose. And obviously, Mr. Parker was happy to see us. *Well, happy to see Laura, at any rate.* We also rode out onto the desert, one of us on my horse and the other on my bike, or riding "double" on Dusty, and we always took a picnic lunch. We had discovered a kind of oasis a few miles from Shafter, with a few scrubby trees and an underground spring providing green grass for Dusty. She liked being out of the corral, and after I went back to school Laura would take her out by herself. Laura said she had a horse back home in Texas, but had to leave him behind when she came out here, and she missed him.

And just why *had* she come out here? I wondered.

When Johnny Dembowski had answered his country's call for men to go off and fight, Laura did not want to stay home and "twiddle her thumbs." So she had learned Morse Code, aware of the need for women to replace men as railroad telegraphers—some in desolate outposts like this one. But with Johnny gone, what did it matter, she said.

She worried about her husband. Weeks and even months went by with no word from him. Though he wrote every day, letters had to be sent through a government post office so as to keep troop movements secret from the enemy. Even if you knew where a fighting man was, you weren't supposed to tell. ("A slip of the lip can sink a ship," Uncle Sam told us.)

Johnny had been gone since the beginning of the war— three and a half long years. Now at last the war was over, and she was expecting to hear any day that he was on his way home. The plan was for Johnny to come here to Shafter, first, then take Laura home to Texas. Of course I wanted her to be happy, but selfishly worried about what *I* was going to do after her husband took my friend away. Would I die of loneliness out here by myself? (Though I never suspected it then, my own future was "about as unpredictable as boardinghouse stew!")

I still spent time with old Mr. McNight, reading those wonderful books he had in his house. He taught me how to act out parts of plays. Macbeth ("All the perfumes of Arabia will not sweeten this little hand") and Romeo and Juliet ("O Romeo, Romeo . . . wherefore art thou, Romeo?") were my favorites.

But nothing could postpone that black day when I would have to go to school.

My argument with my mother about "horrible old Mrs. Hoppe" on that morning had been the worst yet. I had refused to eat any breakfast and sat glumly staring at my plate. Then there was a knock on the kitchen door. Señora Hernandez had brought Nita for me to take to school, as promised. The little girl's shining black hair was pulled severely back and secured in one long, tight braid. Her flowered cotton dress appeared to be new, and so did her shoes and pink ruffled anklets. Her large brown eyes wore a worried look. I could see that both mother and daughter were very apprehensive.

Gripping the little girl's hand tightly, Señora Hernandez confided, "Tiene miedo."

"Oh, no, Nita," I said with as much conviction as I could muster. "No, you mustn't be afraid! You'll like school, really you will! And our teacher, Mrs. Hoppe, is very nice. Muy simpática!"

Having heard all my life that God would punish you for lying, by causing your tongue to turn black and fall out, I was waiting for that to happen.

Taking her hand from her mother I said, "Now, Nita, tell Mamacita that you'll see her later. Okay?"

"Okay." And turning to her mother, she said, "Hasta luego, Mamacita."

I nodded to Señora Hernandez, whose eyes were suddenly filling with tears, and the lady walked briskly down the wooden walkway behind the depot and out of sight.

"From now on, Nita, we are going to speak only English, just like I taught you, remember?"

"Okay." (That seemed to be the one English word she was sure of.)

"Before we go to school, though, would you like to see my room?"

"Okay."

I led Nita down the hall to the little bedroom that my mother had tried so hard to make attractive. I saw immediately that her efforts had been a success, at least in Nita's eyes, which grew bigger as she took it all in: the murals with sun and moon, the forget-me-nots painted on everything, bookcases with books—and *dolls!* She had never seen dolls like those, their diminutive clothes made of silk and chiffon, with beautiful tiny faces, and hair of red, gold, and tawny brown.

"Those are called 'Storybook Dolls' and their stories are told in these books—Little Bo Peep, The Queen of Hearts, Cinderella, Goldilocks, Snow White. I'll tell you what let's do," I said. "Every day after school we'll come in here and read these books, where all the dolls' stories are told. Would you like that?"

Nita reached out her little hand toward Goldilocks. (Why is it that little girls with beautiful black hair always want a flaxen-haired doll?) So I said, "We don't play with dolls like these, Nita. They're just for looking at." She quickly withdrew her hand, as if touching one would burn her fingers. "But someday, after you've learned a lot in school and *earned* it, I'll give you Goldilocks or whichever one you want, and you can keep it for your own."

My mother appeared in the doorway of my room. "They're ringing the school bell," she announced solemnly.

This was too much. I couldn't believe that old bronze bell suspended above the pitched roof of the schoolhouse was actually going to *ring!* But now I could hear it, too. Laura had just gone to bed, after her midnight to 8:00 a.m. shift in the office, and the school was right behind her house. From her bedroom it must have sounded like Big Ben.

"Come on, Nita. It's time to go to school," I said with as much enthusiasm as I could manage.

"Okay," said Nita.

Together we trudged off down the path, past the out-house and across Laura's back yard to the schoolhouse. I had seen it only once, from the outside, the day that Daddy and I were out walking and he showed it to me. Now the big double doors were standing open and Mrs. Hoppe was on the porch, welcoming her pupils for the beginning of the new school year, 1945–46. I led Nita, who was holding onto my hand for dear life, up the steps and through the door. Coming in from a warm, sunlit September morning to the musty gloom of a one-room school that has been closed up tight over the summer was a jolt to the senses.

When my eyes adjusted to the dim light, I looked around. The feeling was much like the first time I walked into the General Store and Post Office: that I had been transported to the Hollywood set of a black-and-white movie being made about the Old West. At the far end of the room was a raised platform, approximately ten feet wide, where the teacher's desk and chair sat in front of a large blackboard on the wall with an eraser tray at the bottom. Next to the blackboard there was an American flag on a pole attached to the wall. The rest of the room was filled with rows of old-fashioned wooden desks, with seats attached, and hinged tops fitted with inkwells, enclosing a space for books and papers. The desks were clearly not designed for the upper grades. In fact, I didn't see any big enough to get my long legs under. (But in one corner of the room was a tall stool, where I supposed unruly pupils would be made to sit with a pointed "dunce cap" on his or her head. I might stake a claim to that!)

The room had few windows, and most looked as though they had never been opened—or washed. Between the windows on one side was a squatty black Franklin stove, the only source of heat in the place, that would glow red in the wintertime and make everyone on that side of the room sweat, while everyone only a few feet away, on the other side, would freeze.

Now that all six of her students had filed in, Mrs. Hoppe was closing the big double doors, making the room even gloomier. Unlike the General Store and Post Office, the schoolhouse had no generator for making electricity, so on dark days, kerosene lamps on the walls would provide the only light.

"Good morning, boys and girls!" said Mrs. Hoppe cheerfully. (Wheeze, snort.)

I led a chorus of "Good morning, Mrs. Hoppe!"

A paper in her hand turned out to be a seating chart. Peering at it, a few inches from her nose, she said, "Now, I'll assign each of you a desk, and I want you to keep that same one all year long. Is that clear?"

Mrs. Hoppe's two little girls, Violet and Dorothy (whom she called "Vi-let" and "Dor-thee"), fell to giggling, and I soon understood why. They knew that you could move around freely anytime you wanted to, because Mrs. Hoppe couldn't see who was sitting where.

Initially, anyway, we were assigned seats according to her chart. Violet Hoppe and Nita Hernandez in the first grade, were assigned seats in the front row, closest to the teacher. Dorothy Hoppe, in the second grade, was assigned to the second row. Donald Thomas, in the fourth grade, to the third row. His sister, Betsy Thomas, in the sixth grade, to the fourth row, and I, in the eighth grade, to the fifth row. I showed Nita where her seat was and whispered to her that I would be able to see her all the time and not to worry. "Just do what everyone else does," I told her.

That morning, and every morning afterward, we began by saluting the flag, which we did standing at attention next to our desks with our hands over our hearts. I looked at Nita, who was standing with her hand over her heart, all right, but not saying anything. I hadn't thought to teach her the Pledge of Allegiance, and made a mental note to do that after school today—at least enough so that she could mumble something along with the rest of us.

After saluting the flag, we all sat down (and I squeezed my eighth-grade body into nothing bigger than a third-grade desk) while Mrs. Hoppe passed out books. They all smelled new, and I figured they were what she had been receiving in those Railway Express cartons. I took one look at mine and my heart sank. Her idea of education was the old 3 R's: reading, writing, 'rithmetic.

I had been reading Byron and Shakespeare with old Mr. McNight. The reader which Mrs. Hoppe handed me looked more like Dick and Jane! Last year, in junior high in Sacramento, we had classes in English composition. Now I had a book on penmanship and a copybook for perfecting O's and strokes all slanted in the same direction. In our class in mathematics last year, we were doing fractions and logarithms. Now I had a book titled, "Let's Learn to Divide!"

I wanted to scream.

The best part of the school day was recess, at the end of every hour. At least it was an opportunity to get out of that grim, airless room for a few minutes. But I thought wistfully of my old classmates, back in Sacramento, hurrying from class to class along the wide halls, greeting friends, talking about boys, homework, clothes, and parties. I sighed.

September somehow dragged on into October, and I became increasingly bored and frustrated. I wasn't learning anything, and Mrs. Hoppe was incapable of keeping order, which made it hard to concentrate. Her own little girls, Violet and Dorothy, were two of the worst offenders. Their favorite trick was hiding from her, which wasn't hard—just stepping in behind the stove would do it—or answering "Here!" when the roll was called, and then sitting in a different part of the room, just to keep her guessing.

Donald Thomas loved to bring in the creepy-crawly things that he collected out on the desert and put them in places where people would find them and start shrieking. He put snakes and tarantulas in the girls' outhouse, so I told him that since he was the only boy in the school, we (the girls) were going to use *his* outhouse from then on. And the time I caught him dipping Nita's long braid into the inkwell on the desk behind her, I walked up and rapped him on the head with my ruler. He *did* pull one trick on Mrs. Hoppe which everyone, including me, thought was hilarious.

Donald had a collection of small desert tortoises that would fit nicely into the palm of your hand. One day he took all the black felt erasers off the tray at the bottom of the blackboard and substituted, instead, one of his turtles about the same size. When Mrs. Hoppe picked it up and tried to erase the board with it, we all burst out laughing. And I have to give Mrs. Hoppe credit for being a good sport. When she discovered her mistake—upon very close inspection—she wheezed and snorted several times.

Then I said, "May we please be excused, Mrs. Hoppe?" and dragged Donald out by the collar. Once outside, I said, "Listen, Donald. You quit this nonsense or I'll tell your dad how you're keeping the other kids from learning anything, and how you're not learning anything *either!*" Donald knew this would mean a trip to the woodshed. And that's when he told me that he couldn't read.

I was shocked. Donald was in the fourth grade, and he had never learned to read! Mrs. Hoppe had just passed him from grade to grade because she didn't know what else to do with him. I knew the younger ones would suffer the same fate because Mrs. Hoppe was either overwhelmed, incompetent, or possibly both.

Something had to be done, both about the shameful level of teaching and the lack of discipline. And so I became a kind of student-teacher and classroom cop, abandoning my own "lessons" and spending most of the day working with the younger children. If I wasn't learning anything, well, others *were*. And that, I told myself, was something.

One day I had an idea that appealed to everyone, including Mrs. Hoppe. I proposed that I should write a *play,* that all the kids should have parts, and we might even put it on for the parents—with costumes and everything!

My mother was astonished at my diligence, when night after night was spent scribbling away at the kitchen table with books and a dictionary. I tried to devise a plot that would fit all six of us, and finally came up with one. It was about a family of hillbillies who had struck it rich (presumably with oil discovered on their land) and now lived in luxury. They even had a Spanish maid. It would not be credible to make Nita one of the children in this otherwise lily-white family, so she had to play the maid. That was too bad, but I couldn't think of any other part for her.

It was a 30-minute, one-act play. I wrote out each of their parts on separate pieces of paper and told the kids to learn their lines by a certain date, when we would begin rehearsals. At first I let them walk through it holding their scripts, but soon they wanted to do without them. The raised platform at the end of the room where Mrs. Hoppe sat was perfect for the "stage." We covered the blackboard with an old window curtain, and pushed her desk out of the way on the night of the performance. People loaned us a few pieces of living room furniture for the set, including a creaky old rocking chair.

Besides the Maid (played by Nita), there were the Two Sisters (played by Violet and Dorothy), the Father (played by Donald), the Mother (played by Betsy), and the Grandmother (played by me). My mother made what costumes we needed, including an adorable little black dress with a frilly white apron and lace headband for Nita. Violet and Dorothy wore their own "Sunday Best" outfits. Donald had a dark-blue suit that Grace had bought him for his grandfather's funeral, and he sported my father's Fedora and a penciled-on mustache. Betsy looked pretty much like her own pudgy self, but I was able to give her a more sophisticated hairdo, and she wore her mother's only pair of high heels. As the grandmother, I wore one of my mother's dresses and a shawl over my shoulders. In lieu of a gray wig, I tied my hair up in a bandanna and had wads of white cotton peeking out from under it. I was also supposed to be quite deaf, and wanted an ear trumpet, but had to make do with the megaphone off the Victrola, held up to my ear.

I gave myself only one line, as the hillbilly grandmother (but made a lot of noise rocking back in forth in the creaky old rocker and saying "Eh?" (holding up my ear trumpet). I will never forget that one line. The father comes home and reports that a friend has been shot. The mother asks where, and the father replies that he was shot in the vestibule. Whereupon, the grandmother exclaims, with a shocked expression on her face, "*In ther VESTER-bule! Mercy me!*"

The play was a hit. The whole town (Population 25, including the Mexican section men) came to see it. Parents ooh'd and ahh'd at seeing their children on the stage. To my surprise, Donald Thomas showed real acting ability. Old Mr. McNight applauded loudly and cried, "Bravo!" several times and then, "Author! Author!"

Some things had been accomplished. The kids had buckled down and pulled together to make this little venture a success, it had given us all (myself included) something different and exciting to do, and I had written a play.

It was my first experience with "live theater." I was hooked, and it was to become a lifelong addiction.

CHAPTER EIGHT

Covering for Daddy

Every few weeks Joe Thomas took the train into Wendover or Elko to buy supplies for the store. He usually asked my father to go along and help him load boxes and barrels into the baggage car and unload them again when they got back to Shafter. I knew Daddy was happy to help out because, for one thing, he and Joe were friends, and for another, it gave him the opportunity to replenish his own "supplies" for the men's outhouse behind the depot, where I knew he was keeping his whiskey.

Although Joe was not a "drinking man," as he always said, he would go into a bar and "hoist a few" with my father while they waited for the train in Wendover or Elko. And that worried me. Often, when he got off the train, I could tell that Daddy was three sheets to the wind.

It was the middle of November now, and it was getting cold in the desert. I wore a heavy jacket and wool pants to school and didn't mind sitting close to the stove most days. In fact, everyone migrated to that side of the room after the roll was taken. (Mrs. Hoppe couldn't see where you were sitting, anyway.)

I had only been home from school a few minutes, one afternoon, when Joe Thomas rapped on the kitchen door, and I could tell by the sound of it that he was angry. I dreaded hearing what he had to say, which was that he and my father had gone into the State Line Hotel in Wendover to "hoist a few" before boarding the train with supplies he had bought for the store. But when it came time to leave, he couldn't get Daddy away from the dice tables. Joe was furious because he'd had to lift all those boxes on and off the train without Daddy's help—even including, he informed my mother, a case of whiskey that my father had bought for himself!

So that particular cat was out of the bag. And now my mother was furious, too. But that wasn't the worst part. At 4:00 Daddy had to go to work and it was nearly that now. After Joe Thomas stormed out of our kitchen, I tried assuring my mother that Daddy would get back before long. In the meantime, I would go into the office and tell Jean that she could go home at 4:00, as usual.

"And what if he doesn't get back?" my mother said through clenched teeth.

"I'll cover for him."

"You can't do that. We'll have to ask Jean to stay."

"No," I said firmly. "She'll report him again."

"Maybe he *needs* reporting," said my mother, in whose view crime deserved punishment. No two ways about it.

"It'll be okay," I said.

"What about Laura?"

I knew that Laura was in Salt Lake on family business and not expected to return much before midnight.

"It'll be okay," I said again.

Little Nita was still sitting in my room with an open book on her lap, the last pages of *Cinderella* as yet unread. I told her that she would have to run on home now, and I would see her tomorrow. She looked disappointed, but did as she was told.

Putting on a casual air, I went into the office at 4:00 and told Jean that my father was going to be a little late, but that she could go home anyway. I would cover for him. She looked suspicious because she had seen Joe Thomas get off the train from Wendover and unload all those supplies by himself, so she had a pretty good idea what had happened. Also, she knew that I was at least as good an operator as she was, and she resented it. *Well, that was just too darned bad.*

Before leaving, Jean handed me the train schedule for the next eight hours. I thanked her and sat down in Daddy's chair. When she was gone I looked at the schedule. A light traffic night. That was a blessing.

When she saw Jean leaving the office, my mother came in, still with fire in her dark eyes. Then she saw me sitting in Daddy's chair and burst into tears. My poor mother! It was clear now that she regretted coming here, regretted putting herself and me into this dismal situation, regretted ever marrying my irresponsible father, and perhaps a few other things, too. But that wasn't going to help now.

All I could say was, "It'll be okay, Mommy." *I sure hoped I was right!*

The telegraph terminal began clicking, and I put on the earphones to listen to what was coming over the wire.

"What's *that?*" There was panic in my mother's voice.

"Nothing I can't handle," I said with a confident shrug. "Routine stuff."

They were orders for the next train, due in fifteen minutes, but I knew what to do. When the clicking stopped, I unlocked my father's "bug" and repeated the message back to EJM, the dispatcher in Elko, signing it GPS, my father's initials. Then the clicking began again with the message: GPS—Who is sending?—EJM.

Rats! The dispatcher knew it wasn't Daddy who sent the message.

My father had told me that each operator has a distinctive touch. "It's like your thumbprint. No two are exactly alike. Anyone who is used to hearing a certain operator sending Morse Code can tell that person's touch from everyone else's."

I answered the new message with another: EJM—my father is out back (and signed it with my own initials)—EES. Then I held my breath. There was a silence, then the answer came back: EES—understood—EJM.

Whew! I could breathe again. But now I had to get the orders up to the train that was approaching. Glancing at the big Regulator clock on the wall, I knew I would have to hurry. Taking a set of order forms from the wooden desk tray, I rolled them into the battered old typewriter and banged out the message on its wobbly keys. Then I tore off the office copy and folded each of the other two into small squares to be attached to the two hoops—one for the engineer, the other for the conductor at the end of the train—and ran outside with them. Now I could see the big black face of the locomotive steaming down the track and heard the WOOO, WOOO, Woop, WOOOOO as the engineer signaled for the crossing at the Nevada Northern tracks. I held up the first hoop at just the level I knew the fireman, crouching between the engine and the tender directly behind, would need it to be. As he put out his arm and caught the hoop, he smiled. He had seen me do this before (but my father was usually standing there, too). When the caboose approached, I saw Mr. Parker holding out his arm to catch the second hoop. He gave me a big grin and waved as the train disappeared out of sight.

My knees were shaking when I walked back into the office, but seeing my mother's puffy, tear-stained face, I smiled, snapped my fingers, and said, "See? Nothin' to it!"

Hours went by, but thankfully there were no more train orders to receive and acknowledge. (I wasn't sure how many more times I could tell EJM that my father was "out back!")

At 10:00 the last "milk run" from the east arrived and Laura was on it. And so—praise the Lord!—was my father. They got off the train together, and I could see that Laura was angry about what he'd done. She was also worried that Jean had been called in to cover for him and knew what that would mean. When she saw me sitting at the desk instead of Jean, she grinned and said, "Well, howdy, Slim. Y'all been busy?"

In bed that night I stared at the luminous stars on the ceiling and thought about what was happening to my little family: My father was in danger of losing his job, my mother was worried and angry, and I hated school. Just when I thought things couldn't get any worse, they did.

In the middle of all this "double, double toil and trouble" (Macbeth) came a letter from my sister with the news that she and her Air Corps lieutenant husband would be coming to spend a whole week with us at Thanksgiving. Since their wedding two years ago they had been living in Texas, where he was stationed.

I dreaded this new development. For one thing, my

My sister in her ROTC uniform

mother and sister had never gotten along together. They were too much alike, I suppose, both being stubborn and strong willed. I loved my sister. She was beautiful, vivacious, and funny. She made everyone laugh with her hijinks and wacky sense of humor. In high school she was always voted the Most Popular Girl, and in her senior year she was given a "commission" in the ROTC as an honorary girl colonel. She was a knockout in her uniform with the short skirt, brass-buttoned jacket, and leather boots. The boys had to salute her, too, which made it all the more fun. When she was voted the Girl

Most Likely to Marry a Millionaire, my mother said she hoped she *would* marry a millionaire—one who could afford a *maid*, because she was such a terrible housekeeper.

I was watching my mother as she wrung her hands over the letter. "Where are we going to put them, George?"

Now, that in itself was a bad sign. My parents had gone from the "Paddy and Rosie" stage to the "Mother and Daddy" stage and were now into the "George and Rosa" stage—the lowest rung on the ladder.

I would gladly have given my sister and brother-in-law my room with the stars on the ceiling, but it only had a single bed, so that wouldn't help. And although my father had been exiled to the sofa since his last escapade in Wendover, giving them the big bedroom would still leave my mother without a place to sleep. The nearest motel was in Wells out on the highway, twelve miles away.

My father suggested the little place next to the General Store and Post Office. Or rather, connected to it. Joe Thomas had built a lean-to for Grace's mother to live in for a few years before she died. It had two rooms: a small bedroom just big enough for the double bed, and an even smaller kitchen with a table and chairs. It also had a hotplate and electric lights that ran off the store's generator. It even had a stall shower on the back porch and piped-in hot water! Joe had been known to rent it out on occasion. He was over his peeve at my father for that day in Wendover, so Daddy could ask him about it.

My biggest worry was what my sister and brother-in-law were going to *do* out here, and why they wanted to come in the first place. Had my mother painted the same rosy picture of Shafter that she did for me before I came? We would soon know, for they were expected on Tuesday's Exposition Flyer from San Francisco.

School was out for a whole week, "so you'll have more time to spend with Sister," my mother said cheerfully. (I would have preferred another week of school, but what choice did I have?) Her biggest worry, now that their sleeping accommodations had been arranged, was what to cook for a Thanksgiving Day dinner. And *how* to cook it, even if she could come by a turkey, which was the next problem. The oven in the little wood-burning stove in the kitchen could hold a chicken but not a turkey.

When our guests got off the train, however, it was obvious that she needn't have worried. Not about food, anyway. Both my sister and her husband were loaded down with shopping bags and boxes, all bearing the logo of stores and gourmet shops in and around San Francisco's Union Square. And one, it turned out, even contained a ten-pound smoked turkey!

That relieved my mother's mind, if not mine.

My sister and I greeted each other with hugs and kisses. She was wearing a heavy winter coat, but she felt like a skeleton inside it.

"You're skinny," I said.

"So are you."

Daddy was unloading their luggage and other things from the baggage car, farther down the track.

"I brought you something. Wait 'til you see."

It wasn't Christmas, so why was she bringing me a present?

My sister and brother-in-law

Her husband, whom I had only seen a couple of times before their wedding, looked awkward and out of place, but I thought he would probably look awkward and out of place anywhere outside the cockpit of his airplane. He was tall, well over six feet, and wearing the "pink" pants of his Army Air Corps uniform with a leather flight jacket. My mother had remarked, after meeting him the first time, that he looked like Rudy Vallee. And he did, sort of.

He shifted a couple of shopping bags from his right hand to his left, in order to shake hands with us. Then he just stood there, looking awkward. Apparently it never occurred to him to go and help Daddy with the things he was unloading from the baggage car.

"Well, so here you are!" said my mother cheerfully. "How wonderful that you could get some leave and come to see us!" This last part was directed at my brother-in-law, who nodded a response and tried a smile on, just for size.

"We *had* to get out of *Texas!*" wailed my sister, abruptly. "You can't *believe* how hot and muggy it is. And the *bugs!* Mosquitos as big as bats!" She turned to her husband. "They'll eat you alive, won't they, honey?"

"Well . . ." said Rudy Vallee.

"Oh, *he* doesn't know," she said, dismissing him with a wave of her hand. "He's always in the nice air-conditioned officers' club."

I saw his back stiffen slightly and the small smile fade. She was deliberately provoking him. Why? Was "something rotten in Denmark?" (Or Texas?)

"Well, let's not stand out here in the cold," said my mother, and we all trooped along after her into the depot.

We passed through the office, where she nodded quickly to Jean, then led us in through the door of the agent's quarters. Soon my father joined us.

"Hello, m'boy!" said Daddy cordially, as he shook my brother-in-law's hand. (He might have stopped for a quick snort in the men's outhouse on the way in.) "I've left the rest of your things on the baggage truck, so we can just take them over to your 'hotel' when you're ready."

My sister said, "Hotel . . . ?"

We explained about the lack of guest rooms in the agent's quarters.

"I tried to tell her," said my brother-in-law. "But she doesn't listen."

"Now, there's no problem at all," said my mother, soothingly. "Evelyn, why don't you take Sister over and show her Joe Thomas's place? But first, she'll want to see your room!"

"Sure," I said with as much enthusiasm as I could manage.

My mother excused herself to put some of the bags and boxes away in the kitchen, exclaiming, "All this food!" That left Daddy to entertain Rudy Vallee as best he could in the living room. The only thing they seemed to have in common was that they both smoked a pipe.

I ushered my sister into my little room at the end of the hall and stood aside while she looked around.

"Good grief!"

"Shh. Don't let Mommy hear you. She tried very hard to—"

"What are those things on the ceiling supposed to be? *Stars?*"

"Yes. They glow in the dark," I explained lamely. "Luminous paint."

"No one but Mother would think of something like *that*." She was digging in her purse for a cigarette. When she found one, she said, "I see you've still got those funny little dolls."

"Uh-huh."

When she struck a match, I noticed that her hand was shaking.

"Well, let's go over to Joe's place."

"What is it, a bar?" she asked hopefully.

"Oh, no."

I explained that Joe Thomas ran the General Store and Post Office and had a place next to it that he rented out occasionally. Passing the baggage truck in front of the depot, my sister picked up one of the boxes and carried it with her as we crossed the tracks. I figured it contained the present she had mentioned.

I had spent all day cleaning the little lean-to and making it as attractive as I could with a tablecloth, a bouquet of dried flowers, and a bowl of fruit. But when I opened the door, and she stepped inside, my sister just stared in silence.

"Hey, it has electric lights and hot water," I said encouragingly.

"Whoop-dee-doo."

"Okay. I'll trade you my room with the stars on the ceiling."

"Thanks, but no thanks."

Her cigarette had a long ash on the end, so I opened the kitchen cupboard and found an ashtray. She ground out that cigarette and immediately lit another, again with shaking hands.

"Where's the bathroom?" She was looking through the door to the bedroom.

"Outside."

"Outside!"

"It's not so bad in the daytime," I said. "And there's a potty under the bed, if you have to get up at night."

She put the box she was carrying on the kitchen table and sat down in one of the chairs next to it. "I brought you a present . . . Open it."

I opened the box.

My sister's sense of humor ran to practical jokes, which had just about driven my mother and me crazy at home in Sacramento. I remember one hinged spoon and another with a hole in the bottom, fake bottles of milk, wooden eggs that you couldn't tell from the real thing until you tried to crack one, and fake "doggie do" left on the carpet when Lucy was a puppy.

She also used to play tricks on poor "Uncle Edwin," who married our mother after our parents were divorced the first time. I was only six years old, and actually sort of liked "Uncle Edwin," who taught me how to play Cribbage. But I went along with the jokes because I thought we were just having fun. We hid his pipe and put salt in his coffee, among other things. Not surprisingly, "Uncle Edwin" was not amused by these antics. I realize now that my sister's goal was to get rid of our stepfather in any way she could, and sure enough, in less than a year he packed his bags and left.

Looking into the box I had just opened I figured that, if this was one of her practical jokes, it was an elaborate one.

"Ice skates!" I said. "That's pretty funny."

"What do you mean?"

"Isn't it a joke?"

"*A joke!* I paid twenty dollars for those things! You always wanted a pair of ice skates, didn't you?"

"Yes, sure. They're beautiful! Thank you!"

"I thought you could use them out here. Isn't it cold in the wintertime?"

"Yes, but you have to have *water* to make ice. In case you

hadn't noticed, this is a desert." And I added, for emphasis, "The Great American Desert."

To my horror, she burst into tears and sobbed, "I just can't do anything *right* anymore!"

I had never seen my sister cry. I didn't know what to do, or say, so I just patted her shoulder reassuringly. When her sobs had subsided, I said, "What's wrong, Sis? Aren't you happy?"

"No! I hate Texas, I hate being married, and I think I hate *him,* too!" She jerked her head in the direction of the depot where we had left her husband.

Although I could think of a few reasons, myself, I still asked why.

"He has no *personality!*" she wailed.

I thought it was a pity she hadn't noticed that before she married him, but I didn't say so.

"It was the uniform," she said. "I fell for a uniform."

She thought it would be fun, being married to an Army officer. All the boys she knew in high school seemed so juvenile when she met this tall lieutenant at a party for pilots training at Mather Field, near Sacramento. Not long afterward he asked her to marry him, and so she did, only a week after graduation. She was just eighteen. Our mother opposed the marriage because, for one thing, the boy was Catholic, and for another, she thought my sister was too young and immature to be getting married. There were pitched battles over it, and in the end my sister married the boy—mainly, I think, to prove that she could be just as stubborn as her mother, even more so. Anyway, in a million years she would never admit that Mommy was right, which she clearly was, in this case. She was right about another thing, too. My sister *was* "selfish and bone-lazy," as she used to say. When an aunt and uncle offered to send her to college, she declined, saying it sounded "too much like work!" Instead, she preferred to marry her tall lieutenant and have an exciting, fun-filled life. Now that dream was in shambles.

When they moved to the Army base in Texas, she thought she would be going to parties and dances and have friends among the other wives. But her husband seemed to spend most of his time in the company of other fliers, and she was "stuck with a bunch of drips who sit around talking about their *babies* all the time!" (After two years of marriage, she was still childless.) When he did come home, her husband criticized her lack of housekeeping skills, even expecting her to keep their apartment clean! Imagine that! It was all so *unfair!*

I didn't know what to say, remembering the vivacious and fun-loving Most Popular Girl in high school, who was nothing like the unhappy young woman she had become. I was shocked at the change in her. Murmuring some words of sympathy, I waited until she finally blew her nose and dried her eyes.

"What do *you* do out here?" she asked.

I told her about my horse, about the school play, about old Mr. McNight, who had such great books, and about how I "hopped freights" with my friend, Laura. She stared at me with dull, swollen eyes.

"Is there any place to get a drink around here?" she asked at length.

I thought about the men's outhouse in back of the depot

with Daddy's stash of whiskey, but decided not to mention it. "You mean, like a bar?"

"Yes. Or a tavern, or something."

Now I thought about Daddy's favorite place, the State Line Hotel in Wendover, but that seemed a long way to go for a drink.

"No, there isn't."

"What? *Nothing?* What's next door?"

I described the General Store and Post Office.

"Do they sell wine or beer?"

I remembered that the section men sometimes drank cervezas, or Mexican beer, when we played pool.

"That'll have to do," she said decisively.

This was worrisome. I had seen her drink too much a couple of times while she was still in high school. Now I realized that, along with our mother's beauty and Teutonic stubbornness, my sister might have inherited our father's alcohol dependence.

She seemed to be reading my mind. "Oh, don't look so worried, *Eeyore!*" (Eeyore was the childhood nickname she had given me because I was often fretful, like the old gray donkey in the "Winnie the Pooh" stories. *Well, who wouldn't be worried, with a family like this?*) "I'm only going to buy some beer! . . . Doctor's orders," she said by way of explanation. "A doctor in Texas said I should drink beer to gain weight."

Then she went next door and bought all the beer Joe Thomas had in stock.

The next day I took her to meet Laura. I thought, being the same age and both young married women, they would get along famously. Instead, they hated each other on sight. For one thing, my sister was used to being the prettiest girl in the room. Laura was too much competition in that department. And then, when she found out she was from Texas, she had to tell Laura how much she *hated* living there, and went on to describe in great detail all those *bugs!* And how it was too hot and humid even to *eat,* so she was wasting away to nothing.

I suggested taking her with me to the corral to feed and water Dusty, but she didn't want to walk that far (she joked about driving to the mailbox in front of their apartment building), and naturally declined to walk down the Nevada Northern tracks with Mommy on her rounds of boxcar counting.

We didn't have much better luck with Rudy Vallee. He didn't seem to want to do anything but sit and study a book on airplanes that he had brought with him. After a few futile attempts at conversation, we just left him to it.

We did have a sumptuous Thanksgiving feast, with the smoked turkey and other delicacies they had brought us from their stopover in San Francisco, and my father was happy to help drink the beer my sister had bought at the General Store and Post Office.

Mercifully, the next day Daddy came in with a telegram he had received over the wire. There was some kind of emergency at the Army base in Texas, and all leaves had been canceled. Our guests would have to return immediately.

I stood with my parents, waving to my sister and brother-in-law as their train pulled out of Shafter. I wondered what would happen to them. The war was over, and soon the lieutenant's enlistment would be up. He was not career Army, but had joined to fight the war, like so many others. In a matter of months, or even weeks, he would be a civilian again. *And* he would be out of uniform, which was the only thing that had made him attractive in the first place. I felt sorry for my poor sister.

There were dark days ahead for all of us.

CHAPTER NINE

Changing Times

Soon after Christmas, the other shoe dropped.

I can't remember a more dismal holiday. My parents were barely speaking to each other. Daddy was drinking more and more on the job, and I seemed unable to stop him, though I stayed with him in the office until 10:00 every night, when my mother would insist that I come in and go to bed.

She sat at her treadle sewing machine for endless silent hours, making new clothes for me for Christmas. You would think she was stitching me a shroud, the atmosphere was so gloomy! I tried talking to her, tried to make her see that her attitude wasn't helping Daddy, though—truth be told— I didn't know if anything would help. My father seemed bent on self-destruction.

We had a four-foot Christmas tree, which we cut ourselves at the little oasis Laura and I had discovered out on the desert with the underground spring. It was not a proper fir tree and not strung with lights, because we didn't have electricity, but we draped it with strings of popcorn and colored paper chains I had made at school, and attached candles to the branches. (I thought it symbolic of our current state of affairs that the candles kept turning upside down and dripping wax on everything, and sometimes setting the paper chains on fire, too.)

When she finished sewing, my mother wrapped my

presents and put them under the tree. There was also a new Storybook Doll in its distinctive pink-and-white polka dot box, ordered from the same department store in Sacramento where she had bought all the others. I bought my father a can of good pipe tobacco that Joe Thomas kept in the glass display case below the counter. Laura was teaching me how to knit, and she gave me yarn and knitting needles so I could make my mother a warm scarf for Christmas.

My sister had sent presents, too, along with a letter saying that a doctor in Texas had told her that she would probably never have any children of her own, and advised her and her husband to think about adopting. My sister was willing, but her husband was not, so she had issued an ultimatum: it was either adoption or divorce. We were told to stay tuned for further developments.

On Christmas Eve all the presents were wrapped and waiting under the tree. Unlike most American families who open their presents on Christmas morning, we always opened ours before going to bed on Christmas Eve. It was an old German tradition, my mother said. But I couldn't vouch for that. She had been known to make up "old German traditions" on more than one occasion.

As I left the office at 10:00, I told my father that I would wait to open my gifts until he came in at midnight, then told my mother what I wanted to do. She sighed, wound up the old Victrola, and cheerlessly played Christmas music all evening. *She was trying but, true to form, she was failing.* When Daddy staggered in at 12:30, she got up from her chair, blew out the candles on the Christmas tree, and went to bed without another word to either of us.

Christmas was bad enough, but New Year's Eve was worse. A lot worse.

I begged my mother to let me stay in the office with Daddy until his shift was over at midnight, and Laura would come on. But she said no; letting me stay up past midnight at Christmas had been a mistake not to be repeated on New Year's Eve. She had assumed her Prussian hausfrau stance to deliver the edict. I think she was secretly jealous of the time I was spending with my father. But with open warfare between them, I was being torn in two. I had to divide my time between my mother and father as best I could, and I felt that he needed me more then she did.

I was filled with foreboding, but did as I was told and left the office at 10:00 that evening. Daddy had been "out back" several times already, and I was afraid of what would happen in the next two hours. Of course I could have slipped into the men's outhouse and thrown the bottles of whiskey down the hole. I thought about it, and even walked by there after leaving the office, determined to do just that, but lost my nerve at the last moment.

I got into bed about 10:30 and tossed and turned until finally falling into a fitful sleep. I dreamed that I was alone in the cab of a runaway freight. Frantically, I pulled at the brake lever, which came off in my hand! Then I tried reversing the throttle, as I had seen the engineers do, but that didn't work, either. We went on hurtling downhill at a frightening speed!

Someone was shaking my shoulder and I woke up with a gasp.

"Slim, you'd better get up and come into the office."

It was Laura, and she was standing over my bed in the darkened room. Apparently, she had tiptoed into the agent's quarters, so as not to wake my mother.

I jumped up, threw a robe over my pajamas, and followed Laura into the office. What I saw there broke my heart. Daddy was slumped over the desk, snoring loudly. The telegraph terminal above his head was clicking wildly with news coming over the wire. There had been a derailment down the line.

I knew that nothing would help him now. I had covered for him, lied for him, and been at his side every minute that I could, *and still I had failed to prevent this.* It was nothing short of a miracle that it was not a head-on collision between a fast-moving freight and a slow-moving passenger train. That much, at least, had been averted by the quick action of the two engineers who had suddenly found themselves on the same track. The engineer of the freight had thrown everything he had into stopping his locomotive before clipping the last car of the passenger train. The other engineer, in turn, had jumped the track in a desperate effort to reach the siding where the orders that he should have received at Shafter had told him to go. My father had passed out before he could relay the orders for the passenger train to take a siding and wait for the freight to pass.

On New Year's Eve the rear car of the passenger train, the club car, was filled with people toasting the start of the first year of peace since Pearl Harbor. It was a miracle that no one was killed, or even seriously injured. Otherwise, my father might have been cited for criminal negligence.

As it was, he was only fired.

The next day, January 1, 1946, after fifteen years with the Western Pacific Railroad, Daddy was formally terminated. He was to be replaced immediately with a new agent, by the name of Archibald Denney, who was being sent out from Salt Lake City.

I had stopped telling myself that things couldn't get any worse, because they always did. Now my father had no job, and we had nowhere to go. My mother's face wore her most caustic *"Now look what you've done, George!"* expression, while packing what belongings we could take with us (wherever we were going). All the furniture, which she had brought with her from our house in Sacramento, had to be left in the agent's quarters, which now belonged to Archibald Denney.

Help arrived from two sources. First, the dispatcher in Elko was persuaded to write a letter for my father, praising his many years of service to the Western Pacific and his unique experience and understanding of railroading (leaving out any reference to his problems with alcohol and his recent termination). There was no doubt in my mind that it was Laura who had "persuaded" the dispatcher to write the letter, nor that she herself had threatened to quit unless he did it!

In any case, it turned out to be a godsend, because Daddy was offered a job with the Nevada Northern as the agent in Ruth, about a hundred miles south of Shafter. Coincidentally, he had been offered the same job a year earlier and turned it down. Even as recently as that, he would have considered it beneath him to take a job with a small, mostly freight railroad like the Nevada Northern. But circumstances had changed.

Then Joe Thomas offered my mother and me the little lean-to attached to the General Store and Post Office as a place to live until we decided what we were going to do. (It had become common knowledge—spread by that "common" Jean McNight—that we would not be going with my father.)

For the present, at least, my mother still had her job counting boxcars, and I still had to go to school, much as I hated it. With a heavy heart, I packed up my books and Storybook Dolls and prepared to move into Joe Thomas's little place. I tried to think positively and recall what I had said to my sister, earlier: "Hey, it's got electricity and piped-in hot water!" It only had one bed, though, which meant that my mother and I would have to sleep together. At least we had a roof over our heads, my mother said gravely.

The Nevada Northern, though largely a freight line, did run a passenger train twice a week down to Ely, which boasted the largest open copper pit in the world, and by extension to Ruth, its small sister city nearby. Daddy boarded the Nevada Northern train at Shafter, the day after he'd been fired by the Western Pacific. My mother stayed out of sight, but I clung to him and cried like a baby.

Looking back, I think he was actually relieved to be free of the responsibility of a family, no matter how much he loved us. I remember thinking, as I watched his train fading out of sight, *some men are just not cut out to be husbands and fathers.* He and my mother had been on a twenty-five-year roller-coaster ride, as the incomparably mismatched couple, and I think both of them were glad that it was finally over. This had been their last hurrah. There would be no others.

The next day my mother and I moved into the lean-to next to the General Store and Post Office, and I thought about what my father had said when I first arrived in Shafter: *Sometimes you just have to make the best of things.* After our relatively large quarters in the depot, it would take some getting used to, but it *was* a roof over our heads, after all.

With Daddy gone, I spent more time with Dusty and my dogs, too, but I still felt lonely. Thank goodness for Laura! What would I do without *her?*

I was pumping up the tires on my bike in the baggage room. The weather had turned warm, for mid-January, and Laura and I had decided to go out for a ride on the desert as we often did, with one of us on my bike and the other on my horse. Dusty was saddled and waiting in the corral while I pumped up the tires on the bike.

I heard a *"Yahoo!"* from inside the office, and then Laura burst through the door, waving a yellow telegram above her head.

"Johnny's comin' home!"

These were the very words I had been dreading. Although I tried my best to be happy for her (and felt guilty for feeling the way I did), I was still reeling from the sudden departure of my father from my little world, and now my best friend would be leaving, too! Her husband was coming to take her away with him.

But that would not happen right away, Laura explained. Johnny planned to come here first, and stay until the Western Pacific found a satisfactory operator to replace her, especially since Mr. Denney was still new on the job as agent.

In my opinion, we could do without Mr. Denney altogether! As soon as he stepped off the train from Salt Lake, I decided I didn't like him. He wore a smug, self-satisfied smile and a tweed jacket with leather patches on the elbows. (Why would a man wear a tweed jacket and a tie out here in the middle of nowhere?) There was also a tweedy, snap-brim cap on his head. Whereas I felt out of place in my little seersucker suit when I arrived in Shafter, Archibald Denney gave the impression that *Shafter* was out of place, not *him!* He didn't use the green eye shade and sleeve garters that my father had worn in the office, either. (Not his "cup of tea," he said.) He put up a NO SMOKING sign on the counter, so Orvy McNight had to leave his cigar outside. And, I thought sadly, the pleasant aroma of the pipe tobacco that I had given my father for Christmas would never drift through these rooms again.

Most shocking of all was the fact that Mr. Denney refused to use Morse Code! ("Old hat," he sniffed. But I secretly suspected that the real reason he didn't like it was because he wasn't very good at it.) He insisted that a tele-phone be installed for all communications, including train orders. Was he so important that he could order the railroad to change everything just to suit him?

I was building up resentment toward him with every passing day. But the first time I saw my mother smiling sweetly and touching her hair in that flirtatious way she had with men—*that* was when I began to hate him.

Now it was *my mother* who hung around the office at night, as I used to do when Daddy was the agent. Often, she didn't come home to our little lean-to across the tracks until late in the evening, after I had gone to bed. "Archie," as she was now calling him, occasionally came with her, after his shift was over at midnight. Then the two of them would sit at the table in the tiny kitchen, drinking hot cocoa. (Mr. Denney, as he told us often enough, was a Mormon, and so he never drank "spirits" or coffee, either.)

Johnny Dembowski got off the westbound Exposition Flyer a week later. Laura had been as nervous as a cat all day, combing her hair every five minutes, and changing her clothes three times. She had even taken a bath, although it wasn't Saturday!

I could see why she loved him. He was as handsome as Laura was beautiful. And he was nice, too. But to my surprise he was from Baltimore, not Dallas. They had met at university and, unlike my parents, found that opposites can indeed attract, and not repel.

I liked Johnny so much that I let him ride Dusty while I was in school and Laura was sleeping. He had not yet adapted to her work-at-night, sleep-in-the-daytime schedule. Johnny loved horses and took excellent care of Dusty, who shied away from him at first. (She may have taken him for a mustang trader.) He marveled that I had managed to break and train a wild horse right off the desert! I modestly said that it really wasn't so hard, but didn't tell him about all the bites and bruises I had suffered in the process!

Sometimes the three of us would go for a picnic, with Laura and Johnny riding double on Dusty's sturdy back, and I riding my bike. Other times they went out hunting by themselves because I was afraid of guns and, anyway, I hated the idea of shooting animals. I took Johnny to meet old Mr.

Laura out hunting

McNight, and the two of them got along famously. I began to hope that the railroad would never find a replacement for Laura, and that she and Johnny would stay forever.

That, of course, was only a dream. One day in February, a young man stepped off the train, carrying a suitcase. The rest of his things were in the baggage car. He announced that he was the new telegrapher, sent out from Sacramento to replace the third-trick operator at Shafter. He looked as dazed as I must have, the first time I set foot on that same platform. After breaking in her replacement, Laura and Johnny packed up their belongings and left.

I stood waving to them long after the red lamps on the observation car were out of sight. Laura and I had cried and hugged each other on the platform, and Johnny had hugged me, too. He thanked me for "looking after Laura," and said that she would miss me even more than I missed her. *Fat chance of that!*

I felt terribly alone with Laura gone. I still had old Mr. McNight and my two dogs for company, and occasionally old Moocher. Then, one day as I trudged slowly home from school, I saw Joe Thomas digging a large hole some yards behind the depot. I walked over to see what he was doing and saw to my horror that it was a grave for the ancient brown dog. My father's prediction had come true. Poor old Moocher had been walking down the track and couldn't hear the train coming along behind him. "He never knew what hit him," said Joe, which was meant to comfort me, I suppose.

But I could not be comforted. I cried myself to sleep that night and many nights afterward.

Sooner or later, things were bound to come to a head between my mother and me. I bitterly resented her growing attachment to Archibald Denney, and even her new interest in Mormonism. He had given her some books to study, which she found "fascinating." So now this, from all indications, was to be her latest religious conversion. Several times, while walking home from school, I heard music coming from the Victrola in the agent's quarters. My mother had suddenly developed a nostalgia for the place, furnished with all our things, and Mr. Denney had told her that she was welcome to come in anytime and use the sewing machine, play the Victrola, etc. Which she did, apparently.

Mr. Denney had a wife, of course. He made no secret of that. He told us, with eyes dramatically cast down, that his wife was at home in Salt Lake City, "dying," and had been for years, poor soul! Like everything else about him, I found this performance sickening, but my mother seemed more interested than ever in Archibald Denney.

I was being openly hostile to him these days and took some pleasure in it.

"What is your wife dying of?" I asked rudely.

Mr. Denney was at our place, eating the lunch that my mother had cooked for him on the little hotplate in the kitchen. (She had never cooked lunch for my father.)

"Asthma," he replied.

"We had a cat with asthma one time, didn't we, Mommy?"

Eager to change the subject, my mother asked, "More soup, Archie?"

"I even named her 'Azz-Ma,' remember?" My mother

was shooting daggers at me, which I ignored. "But she didn't *die* of it. She was hit by a car."

"That's too bad," said Mr. Denney.

Sometimes at night I lay in bed and thought about Daddy and how he had decked the saddle tramp in the bar at the State Line Hotel with his powerful one-two punch. Oh, how I longed to see him do the same thing to Archibald Denney! The next time I was at old Mr. McNight's house he was surprised at how much emotion I put into the reading of Hamlet's speech: "Frailty, thy name is woman!"

I also wished that I had the cunning and the courage that my sister had shown in getting rid of "Uncle Edwin" all those years ago. But I knew that practical jokes would not drive Archibald Denney away. I would have to think of something else, if I could.

I saw my first diesel engine that year. It came through Shafter pulling a freight, and we all turned out to see this new phenomenon that rolled silently along the tracks, coming smoothly to a stop and starting off again with no black smoke, no lurching, no huffing and puffing. And diesels, I soon learned, came in all colors! They were painted with each railroad's individual livery and logos. The Western Pacific engines were yellow and black. When they pulled new passenger cars behind them, the train was called a "streamliner."

But if they were pleasing to the eye, they were offensive to the ear. Their air horns sounded more like trucks than trains—like honking geese compared to mourning doves.

Old Mr. McNight wore a worried look these days.

Diesels were the wave of the future, he said, and they ran on oil. Soon there would be no more need for coal chute operators. His son, Orvy, would be out of a job, too. Diesels didn't need water, either.

A letter came from Daddy, enclosing a picture of the Nevada Northern depot in Ruth. It was two-story, and the agent's quarters were upstairs. He joked that it had "all the inside plumbing that your mother always wanted." A flush toilet and hot water. Even a built-in bathtub!

It sounded like heaven. I began to hint to my mother that I would like to go and visit Daddy sometime soon. Maybe over the Easter vacation.

But I didn't have to wait that long.

One night I was awakened by voices in the kitchen, one of them my mother's.

"I've never heard her say a word against you, Archie," she said, meaning me, obviously.

Nevada Northern depot in Ruth

I couldn't hear what Mr. Denney said in response, but I got up quietly and tiptoed to the door. From there I could see my mother, and she was sitting on Mr. Denney's lap! I had to force myself to stay out of sight and not go storming in and telling that horrible man to get out of our house! Instead, I waited until the next morning, after I had carefully rehearsed what I would say to my mother. Then I screamed at her, accusing her of driving my father away with her cold-hearted, holier-than-thou attitude, and now, like some faithless Jezebel, she was cozying up to the very man who had stolen his job! I think I also repeated my dramatic reading of Hamlet's "Frailty, thy name is woman!" and added that if she didn't change her ways, I would go and live with my father!

I was stunned by her reply. "That might be the best thing for all of us."

In fact, she went on to inform me, I might as well know that she intended to *marry* Mr. Denney! She had already started divorce proceedings against my father. When I reminded her that Mr. Denney already *had* a wife, back in Salt Lake City—and, as far as I knew, Mormons were no longer *polygamous*—she brushed that aside as a temporary obstacle. The present Mrs. Denney was not expected to live very long, poor soul.

My mother started packing my trunk and sent a wire to my father. I told Mrs. Hoppe that I would not be returning to school the next week and made my own preparations for leaving. Daddy's reply to the wire had said that I could bring my two dogs and my bicycle, but not Dusty, of course. That caused me the most pain of all.

The day before I left, I gave my whole Storybook Doll collection to Nita. They had all been given to me by my mother, and I didn't want them anymore.

When I couldn't put it off any longer, I went to say goodbye to old Mr. McNight.

"Parting is such sweet sorrow," he intoned, wiping his eyes.

Then I walked out to the corral and sat on the top rail while Dusty munched the apple I had brought and nudged my pocket, looking for another. I hugged her soft neck. Her coat was sleek and shiny from the good food she was getting now and from the daily brushing. Then I led her outside the corral, where she waited beside the shed for me to get out the saddle. Instead, I slipped the halter off and said, "Goodbye, Dusty. You're free now!" She didn't seem to understand, so I slapped her on the rump and said, "Go on, girl! Get out of here! And stay away from mustang traders!"

A few minutes later, I watched Mr. Denney loading my grandmother's little trunk, my bicycle, and the two animal crates containing Lucky and Lucy, onto the baggage car of the Nevada Northern train that would take me to my new home above the depot in Ruth. Then I picked up my little cardboard suitcase and boarded the train.

It was the end of an era, in more ways than one. I was leaving this place that I hated at first, but learned to tolerate because I had friends like Laura and old Mr. McNight, and a horse to ride. Diesels were replacing the steam trains that I had grown up with, and even the exalted Exposition Flyer would soon die and be reborn as a sleek new streamliner called the California Zephyr.

A California Zephyr. *Courtesy the California State Railroad Museum*

Three hours later I watched my father unloading all my possessions once more. When the dogs had been fed and watered and shut up in the baggage room, where they howled in protest, Daddy took me upstairs to the agent's quarters.

It was just as he had described it. But he had left out one very important thing: my grandmother was there.

My father was forty years old when I was born, so his

mother had always seemed ancient to me. She had never known her own father, who was killed (as a Confederate soldier), in the last battle of the Civil War in 1865, when she was only three months old. Her mother later remarried, giving young Laura Belle a wealthy but dour and extremely strict stepfather who virtually made her a prisoner in an ivory tower. It was said that he always shielded her from view in public, even standing in front of her seat in a carriage, so that men couldn't see and admire her. She was never allowed to mingle with people her own age, male *or* female. *No wonder she turned out to be such a sourpuss!* But how she was able to meet and marry the zany George (alias Lord D'Anjou) Smith, I never found out.

Now her heavy, black, old-fashioned shoes made a "clunk-clunk-clunk" sound on the bare wood floor as she came to the door of the agent's quarters. You could tell she wasn't any happier to see me than I was to see her. She and my mother had always hated each other, mainly because my mother would not have her around. And I could understand why. She was a bitter old lady whose negative attitude and constant carping would drive any sane person crazy. One of the few people who could abide her was my father, which is why she was there, on her semi-annual pilgrimage to the only remaining relatives who would still have her. During the other six months of the year she lived in Iowa with her daughter, my father's sister Rachel.

Finding my grandmother in residence in the depot at Ruth dealt a serious blow to my hopes for a new and better life.

Over Grandma's thunderous pronouncement that dogs

belonged *outside,* Daddy said that Lucky and Lucy could live upstairs with us. That was one small triumph, anyhow. There weren't many.

Once I tried talking to her about my grandfather, who Daddy told me had fled a boring job in his father's bank and sailed off to Paris as the dashing Lord D'Anjou.

"Stuff and nonsense," she sniffed. "Horse feathers!"

She had been married to the man for fifty years, she said, and there wasn't a word of truth in that old yarn. When I defended the legend by saying that Daddy had one of the calling cards that Lord D'Anjou had printed before he left, she said, "Have you ever *seen it?*" And I was forced to admit that I hadn't.

Grandma enjoyed poking holes in other people's dreams, probably because she didn't have any of her own.

Another time, I brought out an old picture album that I had found in the bottom of her little trunk that had come with me from Sacramento to Shafter, and now to Ruth. When I showed her the album she seemed pleased, at first. *But Grandma was never pleased about anything for very long!*

"Is this you, Grandma?" I asked, pointing at a picture of a young woman in a beautiful dress and hat.

"Let me see . . . Oh, yes. I loved that bonnet."

"You sure were a pretty girl, Grandma."

"Hmph. Much good it did me. My stepfather thought that beauty was a curse. Worse than that. He said it was the work of the devil."

I pointed to the picture of another pretty young girl. "Who's this?"

My grandmother, Laura Belle

My father's sister, Rachel

"My only daughter, Rachel. She must have been about your age, maybe a little older, when that was taken."

Yes, I could see a strong family resemblance between Daddy and my Aunt Rachel. I thought she looked a little like me, too, except for her naturally curly hair. Mine was straight as a string.

"She was a redhead, like her father," added Grandma.

So, the dashing Lord D'Anjou had red hair! I couldn't say why that made him even more interesting, but it did!

I pointed at another picture. "And who's the good-looking young man, holding a baby?"

"My stars! Don't you know your own father?"

I looked again and asked, "Which one is my father?"

"The young man, of course!"

The child appeared to be a boy, not my sister or myself, so I asked, "Whose baby is he holding?"

For the first time my grandmother's stern look softened a little. *She almost smiled!*

"Mine. That's my youngest son, Gaylord."

"Daddy looks about twenty years older than—"

"Well, he was. I had three grown children when little Gaylord came along." And by way of explanation, she added, "We came into a sum of money, some time after the other children, so Father and I decided on having another baby."

I had always heard that Daddy's younger brother Gaylord, far from being "decided on," had been quite a "mid-life surprise" to his parents. But being the baby, he had been indulged and pampered all his life. And, if you believed the gossip, had come to a bad end as a result.

My father and baby Gaylord

He was supposedly a dead ringer for Errol Flynn and worked as the star's stand-in double for many of his films in the 1930s and early 1940s. Like the actor himself, he was extremely handsome, the same age and height (6 feet, 2 inches), dyed his hair and grew a pencil-thin mustache to add to the illusion. Many a movie fan mistakenly took him for the real thing, and my uncle obligingly signed their autograph books with, "Best wishes, Errol Flynn."

I never met Gaylord Smith, who died young and whose line of work was not considered a respectable way of making a living. But it was more his scandalous lifestyle (like Errol Flynn's) that made him the black

My uncle Gaylord

sheep of the family. Some even said it was a blessing that Uncle Gaylord's life was cut short when his speeding sports car jumped the curb and crashed into a tree one night on Sunset Boulevard.

I wondered how bad you had to be before you were branded a black sheep. *You couldn't exactly call my father a fleecy-white one!*

Then another picture, of a handsome young man apparently panning gold in a stream, caught my eye. It was a little blurry but still recognizable and I knew immediately who it was. "Wow! He really *does* look like Errol Flynn!"

The stern look came back into my grandmother's face, and she snapped, "Well, I don't know anything about *that.*"

As she stormed off to the kitchen in her clunky shoes, she muttered, "If a body hasn't anything better to do than sit around looking at old pictures, then she had better get herself out here and start shelling the peas for supper!"

I sighed as I closed the album and put it back in the little trunk. There would never be any love lost between Grandma and me, but I could take a little comfort in the fact that her yearly visits never lasted more than a few months. Soon she would be going back to her home in Iowa, and Daddy and I would be left in peace.

But it didn't quite work out that way.

Daddy told me that he had been to see the principal of the Ruth School—or rather the principal, Mr. Penn, had been to see *him.* Mr. Penn's wife, Lena, was Norwegian and in the habit of receiving a wooden bucket of herring every few weeks from relatives in Oslo. The fish arrived in Ruth via the Railway Express, and Mr. Penn would come into the office in the depot to get them. He had been in recently, and Daddy had told him that I was coming.

I dreaded starting the eighth grade over again in Ruth. When I did, I found that I was behind in subjects like history and geography. But my knowledge of Shakespeare and classical literature, thanks to old Mr. McNight, all but astounded my teachers!

And, to my delight, I found that Ruth was actually a *town,* with hundreds of people. There were cars on the streets, grocery and clothing stores, and even a movie theater! Unfortunately, this being Nevada, there were also taverns, bars, and casinos.

It didn't take much to figure out why Daddy was looking so cheerful these days. In addition to being freed from an unhappy marriage, he was in his element every night in the bars and gambling houses. His hours in the depot here were not what they had been in Shafter. The Nevada Northern was too small a railroad to require three shifts, or "tricks," over a twenty-four-hour day. My father was the only operator, and his hours were arranged to accommodate the small number of trains coming and going, plus keeping the Railway Express office open during the daytime. He also had weekends off.

Many nights Grandma would send me down to "those establishments," as she called the bars and casinos, to bring Daddy home. I usually found him at the Roulette wheel or the dice tables, a large glass of whiskey by his side. I have said that my father was the world's best poker player. The opposite was true with any other form of gambling, and now he was the one who owed money to everyone. My grandmother complained of not having enough for groceries, and I had to use my allowance to buy dog food for Lucky and Lucy.

I began to find him more and more often in the company of a voluptuous blonde when I went looking for him among the crowds in the taverns. There were even whispers about it around school. Imagine my horror on learning that she was the principal's Norwegian wife! Lena Penn shared Daddy's love of gambling, and liked to stay out late while her "hossbund" graded papers. (Mr. Penn was the math teacher in addition to being the principal.) At the end of an evening or more often, early in the morning, she would ask my father to walk her home, up the dark canyon where she and Mr. Penn lived. And Daddy, being the chivalrous gentleman that he was, would do it. Anyone could have seen them, and did.

I began thinking, again, that things couldn't get any worse. But, as usual, I was wrong.

Daddy had staggered home from one of his nights out with Mrs. Penn, and found, to his surprise that it was not Saturday, as he had thought, but Friday. Not his day off, but a day when he should have been in the office, taking train orders coming in over the wire. There had been another accident.

I never found out if there were casualties connected with this one, but the next day Daddy no longer worked for the Nevada Northern.

Now, it seemed no railroad in the country large enough to have two trains running in opposite directions would take a chance on hiring my father. He was finished as a telegrapher, the only job he had known since he was a stockbroker, back in 1929.

My grandmother was dismayed, of course, but, to her credit, refrained from heaping hot anger or cold contempt on Daddy, as my mother would have done. For my part, I sat numbly wondering what was going to happen now, after this latest disaster.

"I guess we should get in touch with Mommy," I said, supposing that I would have to go back to Shafter.

My father and grandmother exchanged looks, but neither said anything. I studied their faces and braced myself for more bad news.

"We can't, Sweetheart. We don't know where she is."

"What do you mean?"

"She's gone!" hissed my grandmother. "Run off with some no-account—"

Daddy held up his hand. "Mother, please."

Turning to me, he explained that his last letter to Mommy had come back marked, "Moved. Left no forwarding address." Joe Thomas had been good enough to write him a note along with it, saying that she had gone to Salt Lake City with Mr. Denney, who had been terminated by the Western Pacific. Joe had no further news about either of them.

I saw one glimmer of hope in all this. "Well, then, I guess I'll just go wherever you're going, Daddy."

Again my father and grandmother exchanged looks. *Now what?*

"I'm sorry, Punkin. I don't know where I'm going. You've got to go to school, and with my own future up in the air like this, I couldn't expect you to tag along!"

"Oh, but I *want* to! I turned fourteen last month."
(Nobody had remembered my birthday.) "I don't need to
go to school! I'll—"

"You've got to tell her, George," interrupted my grandmother.

"Tell me what?" I could hear the panic in my own
voice.

"You're going to Iowa. Your aunt Rachel wants you to
come and live with her and Uncle Karl. Grandma's going
to take you home with her."

This was worse than all the calamities I could have
imagined. *Iowa!* Where in the world was *that?* It might have
been in another galaxy as far as I knew!

"But you can't take *them!*" My grandmother was pointing to the sleeping dogs at my feet. "Your Uncle Karl raises
purebred Cocker Spaniels, and I can tell you right now that
he wouldn't want those two mongrels around."

In fact, my grandmother went on to inform me, Uncle
Karl didn't tolerate any nonsense from dogs *or* children,
being very strict with both! I would certainly have to watch
my "p's and q's" around *him,* she warned grimly.

Just as I had on the day I arrived in Shafter, I began
thinking about running away. I would take my two dogs
and sneak off, after everyone was asleep!

But where would I go?

There is little more to tell about those dark days. My
father said he would try to find a good home for my dogs,
so I said a tearful goodbye to my dear old friends, unable to
bear the soulful look in Lucy's eyes. Daddy bought bus tickets to Iowa for my grandmother and me, with money he'd

managed to borrow somewhere. This time I wouldn't be going by train and traveling on a pass. Daddy didn't work for the railroad anymore.

I felt like a condemned prisoner standing on the gallows, waiting for the trap door to open under my feet. I wasn't an orphan. I had two perfectly good parents! But I had been abandoned by both of them, and now I was being shunted off to live with strangers in some God-forsaken place called Iowa.

Nothing could have convinced me, in that blackest hour of my young life, that this was the best thing that ever happened to me.

But it was.

CHAPTER TEN

Going Back

After my freshman year at the University of Iowa, I tried persuading Uncle Karl that I was old enough, and responsible enough, to answer one of those "You drive it. We pay for the gas" ads for people to deliver cars to either coast from the factory in Detroit.

Though I was barely nineteen and had never driven on a four-lane highway (they didn't have such things in Iowa), I'd had a driver's license since I was fourteen, and I was a good driver—hadn't he taught me himself? In the end I had my way, as usual. Dear old Uncle Karl, in whose presence others trembled, was putty in my hands!

"They must be desperate for drivers," he observed when I handed him the letter, in answer to my application to drive a car to the West Coast. Bring a valid driver's license and come to Detroit immediately to pick up a brand-new 1951 Chevrolet, it said. I was thrilled! And if it turned out to be a convertible, I would be ecstatic!

My uncle was right, of course. They *were* desperate for drivers. The war had been over for five years, and despite the onset of a new "skirmish" in Korea, manufacturers were still trying to keep up with the demand for cars from a public that had been deprived of them for so long. America had "New Car Fever."

Passing muster with General Motors was a snap, however, compared to getting Uncle Karl's approval. Being an economics professor, he naturally put great store in fiscal responsibility, which included precise record keeping. First, he gave me a pocket-sized ledger in which I was to record every penny that I spent for gas, when and where I bought it and, at each stop, to compute the gas mileage. It would be good training for when I had a car of my own, he said.

Next, he took me out to the garage where his new Dodge was parked, and instructed me to back it out and change a tire! I had to jack the car up, take off the hubcap, and loosen the nuts, pull the tire off the rim, and then reverse the process, using the spare in the trunk. I wondered if I would be graded on how well I did on this test, with graduation from the university riding on it! (I was already on thin ice with my science requirement.)

On to the terrors lurking under the hood! Service stations were not doing a proper job these days, he warned. Better to do it yourself. Check the oil to see that it was up to the "full" line. Only loosen the radiator cap to view the water level when the engine was cool, never hot. Look around for loose wires, and see that the battery cables are securely attached. Inspect the spark plugs for any signs of corrosion. Check the windshield wipers. (A new car should have new wiper blades, but make sure they work.) A woman alone out on the highway must have a flashlight with new batteries and flares in case of trouble. I had to light a flare, just to prove I knew how do it.

I was studying to be an architect, not a service station attendant! Was all this really necessary, I wondered? It was, because that was Uncle Karl, through and through: conscientious, sober, and meticulous in all things.

You would have thought my father and Uncle Karl had been born on different planets. Uncle Karl was a "social" drinker, and then little more than the one glass of imported sherry that he sipped every night before dinner. His gambling was limited to a game of Canasta with Aunt Rachel and a couple of neighbors on a Sunday afternoon. And I used to say that it would take an act of Congress to get him out of the house in the evening. In the five years that I lived under his roof he had been coaxed out only once. That was to see *Henry V,* a 1944 film starring Laurence Olivier that finally made it to Iowa City three years later.

The love of Uncle Karl's life was Daddy's sister Rachel. I cannot imagine that he ever looked at another woman. They were one more study in contrasts, those two, being opposites in every way. (But, like Laura and Johnny Dembowski, it worked!) He was quiet and contemplative, modest, and even shy. She was outgoing, fun-loving, and sometimes even a little outrageous. On a hot day she might fling off all her clothes and walk around the house in the nude. Once I came in with a couple of girlfriends and found her running the vacuum, stark naked except for a small apron tied around her waist. She was not embarrassed in the least. (But I was!)

It was clear to me, the first time I met my aunt Rachel that she and Daddy came out of the same mold. They were both fun loving and occasionally a bit outrageous (although I never saw my father fling off his clothes and pick up a vacuum cleaner). Of course, they came by it naturally, as the offspring of that fun-loving and equally outrageous Lord D'Anjou, alias George Smith.

The missing ingredient in the otherwise perfect union of Uncle Karl and Aunt Rachel was a family. I never heard the whole story, but I knew it concerned a tragic accident early in their marriage, which left her unable to have children. They tried to fill the void in their lives by taking in other people's children when the opportunity arose. Another niece had come to live with them some years before I did and under much the same circumstances. They had also offered to take my older sister into their home and send her to college, which she thought sounded "too much like work," and opted to marry her Rudy Vallee look-alike instead. So, when I fetched up on their doorstep in February of 1946, shivering and on the brink of exhaustion after three days and two nights on a Greyhound bus, they couldn't have been happier.

The next step in preparation for my car trip to the West Coast was selecting the route. Uncle Karl had gone to the Automobile Club and brought home a stack of maps, and was now laying them out on the dining room table. In those days there were really only two ways to drive between the midwest and California: "the southern route" along Route 66 to Los Angeles, and the "northern route" through Salt Lake City to San Francisco. Since my destination was San Jose, where the car was to be delivered, the latter was the best choice. Uncle Karl carefully marked it out for me with a thick blue pencil.

Finally, all that remained was to buy me a one-way train ticket to Detroit, and for both of them to come down and see me off. At the station, Uncle Karl slipped a crisp new hundred-dollar bill into my purse, though he had already given me more than I needed. With Aunt Rachel wiping away tears, he waved his big white handkerchief and blew his nose as the train pulled out. You would have thought I was leaving forever—even though I had promised to be back in plenty of time to register as a sophomore at the university in the fall.

On the train a good-looking young man struck up a conversation with me, and later suggested taking me to dinner when we got to Detroit. I thanked him but said that I had a boyfriend who was in the Navy and stationed at Great Lakes (which I thought was somewhere in that vicinity). I even hinted that I might be on my way to see him there. I said I had promised, when he left, that I would not date anyone else while he was away. I have no idea what made me say that. The boy was just someone I had met in Spanish class and dated a few times before he joined the Navy in order to avoid being drafted. He looked quite handsome in his uniform and had sent me a snapshot to prove it. The picture was still in my wallet, so I got it out and showed it to the man on the train, just to prove a point.

It was a terrible blow to all us freshman girls, newly introduced to the great pool of college men, only to find the pool suddenly drying up when war broke out in some place we'd barely heard of, called Korea. It was also disheartening to see this country back at war after only five years of peace since World War II had ended. But then, Korea was being called a "police action," not a war. That, at least, was some comfort. (But not to girls without dates on Saturday nights!)

The situation was so depressing that a couple of my girlfriends and I finally decided that, if all the boys we knew were either being drafted into the Army or volunteering in another military service, maybe we should join up, too. "If you can't fight 'em, *join 'em!*" became our motto.

The next question was, which service? I suggested the Air Force (formerly, the Air *Corps*), because I thought it would be fun to be an air traffic controller, and women in the Air Force could do that. Jeanine said she didn't like airplanes, and so preferred the lady Marines. Carrie liked the Navy because they had good-looking uniforms and blue was her best color. We did agree on one thing, however. No matter where we went, we would go together. "All for one and one for all!" cheered the Three Musketeers.

Final exams were coming up in a week, which meant we had to act quickly. Iowa City had no military recruiters, the closest ones being in Cedar Rapids, twenty-five miles to the north. So, on a bright May morning the three of us cut our classes and without even telling our parents, boarded the Interurban (known affectionately as the "Vomit Comet"), a little one-car train that lurched and swayed along the tracks between the two cities.

We were filled with the prospect of finally doing something exciting, after so many dull weeks of doing nothing, and chattered about "joining up" all the way to Cedar Rapids. We soon noticed that a young woman sitting across the aisle from us, nicely dressed in a business suit and high heels, was listening intently to what we were saying. A few minutes later she leaned over and asked what we were going to do, so we told her. Her next question was, "What for?"

Not wanting to tell her anything like the truth (which

was that we were bored with our social lives and didn't feel like taking final exams the next week, either), we emphasized the patriotic angle. We explained that each of us was going to take a desk job and "release a man for active duty," like it said on the recruiting posters. We must have sounded convincing (and might even have convinced ourselves in the process). She told us that she was a secretary in Cedar Rapids, lived in Iowa City, and took the Interurban to work, as she was doing that day.

"Would you mind if I came along with you?" asked the young woman, whose name was Anne Tilley. (We dubbed her Tillie the Toiler, after the comic strip, and because she had a job.) The more the merrier, we said.

"All for one, and one for all!" cheered the (now) Four Musketeers as we got off the Interurban and marched toward the Federal Building.

Once inside, the first door we came to was the Marine recruiting office. The young man there shook his nearly shaved head and said Carrie (who measured 4'9" tall) was too short. He explained that you had to be 4'10". Next we tried the Navy. The man in blue was very sorry, but Carrie was too short. He looked hopefully around at the rest of us, who were much taller, but we gave him our "one for all, and all for one" speech, and left. The Air Force was more receptive, and even measured Carrie at 4'10"—not 4'9"! Gleefully, we began filling out the papers, but when the recruiter looked them over he said, "Oh, three of you girls are under twenty-one. You'll have to get your parents to sign for you."

We were crushed. Prospects were slim that my friends'

fathers would sign for them and even slimmer that Uncle Karl, as my guardian, would sign for me. Tillie the Toiler, on the other hand, was over twenty-one and therefore needed no parental permission. The last we saw of our newly minted Fourth Musketeer, she was being sworn into the Air Force. The rest of us took the Interurban back to Iowa City and began studying for final exams.

The car I was going to drive to California turned out not to be a convertible, but a classy little black Chevrolet coupe with imitation leather seats and a gear shift on the steering column. It would be mine for the next ten days— the time allowed for turning it over to the new owner in San Jose.

The only problems I encountered in driving were errors in judgment (my own). Negotiating three-and-four-lane highways proved to be trickier than I thought, and required getting into the passing lane only *after* making sure there were no other cars there. Before figuring that out, I had dirty looks and loud honks on the horn from other motorists. Thankfully, there were no flat tires, but there was a small fire in the ashtray. (I had picked up the "sophisticated" habit of smoking during that first year in college.)

The route Uncle Karl had mapped out for me started in Detroit, where I would pick up the car, then ran due north, through Michigan, and west into Minnesota. I had promised Aunt Rachel that I would stop and pay a call on Glanville Smith, a favorite cousin of both hers and my father's. The three of them were born in St. Cloud, Minnesota, and grew up there together. Cousin Glanville still lived in nearby Cold Spring, in a house called "Railway

View." (I wondered if it really had a view of a railroad, which would make it all the more interesting to me!) Aunt Rachel had written to say that I would be passing that way and would like to stop and pay my respects. His reply was an enthusiastic invitation to lunch.

When I got to Minnesota, and the town of Cold Spring, I had no trouble finding "Railway View," just by following the tracks through that tiny burg of fewer than two thousand hardy souls. (Cold Spring was aptly named for "cold springs and much colder winters," Aunt Rachel had told me.) But in the summertime it was lovely. Glanville Smith's home was like no other I had ever seen, for he was a gravestone cutter, among other things—most notably, a writer of children's books. I still have one of them: *The Adventures of Tippy,* or *The Adventures of Sir Ignatius Tippitolio, Better Known to the World as Tippy, Proprietor of Tippitolio's Grand Imperial Hotel Oriella.* To my knowledge, he never married nor had any children of his own, which I thought was odd for an author of books for children. But in a clipping that Aunt Rachel showed me, it said that neighborhood kids would gather at his house on a Saturday night for "a story, ice cream, and piano duets" with him. I have recently learned that Glanville Smith was really a cultural jack-of-all-trades—that besides being an author and a gravestone designer, he was also a poet, an architect, composer, singer, musician, journalist, naturalist, historian, conservationist, and famous letter writer. His articles appeared in the *Atlantic Monthly* and *National Geographic,* and another of his books, *Many a Green Isle,* about a research trip through the West Indies, is still in print today.

The lot next door to his house held a jumble of grave-stones, all in some state of cutting or repair. I had never realized before that grave markers could be so beautiful. Cousin Glanville was a real artist.

We had lunch on a table set in a charming little rose arbor in his garden. I felt quite grown up when he offered me "a very small glass of sherry to start." (I had never been invited to join Uncle Karl in his nightly aperitif.) The main course was something called Bucks County Tomato Gravy, for which he obligingly wrote out the recipe on a 3 x 5 index card when I asked him how to make it. I still have the card, and occasionally make Bucks Country Tomato Gravy as a reminder of that day. The directions are written in his bold, distinctive hand and colorful prose, calling for frying the tomatoes "in a good lively heat," and then covering them with "as much cream as conscience will permit."

It was such a pleasant afternoon, spent in his quirky little house and garden, in full view of all those beautifully carved headstones on one side and the railway on the other, that I found it hard to say goodbye to Cousin Glanville.

As I was leaving, he asked if I had driven through St. Cloud and seen the building, which was no longer a bank, where my great-grandfather, "J. G." Smith, had been the president. I said no, but told him Daddy's story about his father, "J. G.'s" son, who fled that very bank and a dull career with his "stuffy old man" by changing his name to Lord D'Anjou and sailing off to Paris, where he lived until his money ran out, a year later.

Cousin Glanville knew that story, of course, but he had not heard about the "three drops of royal blood" that my

My great-grandfather's former bank in St. Cloud, Minnesota

grandfather professed to have, nor that I was the "Last Lady D'Anjou," according to tradition. "Your grandfather had a puckish sense of humor," he said. *I could believe that!* After leaving Cold Spring, I drove back through St. Cloud and past the imposing structure that had been "J. G.'s" bank. I had to smile, picturing the dashing Lord D'Anjou escaping that great pile of bricks and his "stuffy old man," if only for a year.

The route that Uncle Karl planned for me ran through Salt Lake City, as I have said, and on into Nevada. I was anxious to cross the Salt Flats before dark on the day I got there, and it was dusk by the time I pulled into Wendover. I didn't really want to stay there, with its many unpleasant memories—like the barroom brawl Daddy had started there six years ago on V-J day—but I did manage to avoid the State Line Hotel by taking a room in a shabby little motel a block away. Uncle Karl would have been appalled at my choice. It was so flea infested that I hardly slept at all, and left at 3:00 the next morning.

When the sun came up I was cruising along the highway in Nevada. The next town on my map was Wells, where I thought I would stop for breakfast. But before I got that far I spied a tiny, arrow-shaped sign off on the shoulder that read:

SHAFTER 12 mi.

The arrow was pointing away to the east. There were no cars coming in either direction, so I skidded to a stop and made a sharp left-hand turn onto a sandy road, once graded, but not much wider than the tire tracks that I followed into the distance. I bumped along for what seemed like more miles than the twelve indicated on the sign, through blowing sand and tumbleweeds, across ditches, and braking to miss jackrabbits that jumped up in front of my car. What if I should run over a sharp arrowhead, like the ones I used to collect by the hundreds out here? I was praying that I would not have a flat tire on this God-forsaken stretch.

Then I could see them. Still the tallest structures anywhere on the horizon: the old water tower and the coal chute at Shafter.

I pulled in behind the depot and got out of the car. My mother's garden, once so carefully tended, was a jumble of tumbleweeds. The outhouse, down the path to the left, was lying on its side. I walked around the depot to the platform in front. The big double doors on the baggage room were closed and padlocked. Posted on the door to the telegraph office was a sign that read:

NO TRAINS

What did it mean? No trains today? Or ever? I peered into the gray windows of the office. There was no one at the desk—my father's desk, where so much of my time was spent beside him, except on that last, fateful night. I turned away.

Shading my eyes against the glare of the sun, by this time higher off the eastern horizon, I tried to see what lay across the tracks. Milepost No. 766, now splintered and faded, was barely legible. The General Store and Post Office was still standing, and against all odds, the roof had withstood another five winters, too. I crossed the tracks in the very spot where I had crawled under a moving freight train, with my father waiting on the other side, ready to pull me up onto the platform and tan my hide.

The General Store and Post Office was closed, as indicated by the sign on the door. I took a handful of tissues out of my bag and wiped a spot on the grimy front window until it was clean enough to see inside. I thought I saw a dim light coming from Joe Thomas's living quarters in the back, but when I knocked, there was no answer. The pool table, now covered with a white sheet, still stood in the middle of the store. And there was the little braided rug on the floor that had been put down for Moocher to sleep on at night. The sight of it brought back the pain of watching Joe Thomas digging a grave for the poor old brown dog.

Had Shafter become a ghost town? Having come this far, I had to find out. Looking down the Nevada Northern tracks I could see there were no boxcars dropped there, and no one to count them, either, I supposed. The section men's houses still looked occupied, but I reserved a visit to them for later, if at all. I had a higher purpose in mind. I wanted to see old Mr. McNight, if he was still around.

When I approached his little railroad tie house, I saw a thin wisp of smoke coming from the chimney. At this time of year the stove would not be used for heat, so he (or someone) must be cooking on it. I approached the front door with trepidation. What if he didn't remember me? I had certainly changed since the last time he saw me, when, as a gangly girl of thirteen I had come to bid him a tearful farewell.

Standing on the doorstep, I heard his splendid voice, still

strong and resonant: "O! pardon me, thou bleeding piece of earth, that I am meek and gentle with these butchers—"

He stopped when he heard my knock. There was a pause, then the door opened, and I laughed and said, "Thou art the ruins of the noblest man that ever lived in the tide of times . . . Julius Caesar, Act Three."

He looked just the same, the white hair still full above the handsome face with the crinkly brown eyes. He stared at me for a moment, then said, "Bless my soul! Is it Lady D'Anjou?" (He had never called me anything else.)

"Hello, Mr. McNight!"

"I thought you would come back one day."

"You did?"

"Well, hope springs eternal in the human breast."

"Alexander Pope."

His broad smile told me how pleased he was to see me. He invited me into his "humble abode," and begged me to share the meal he was cooking on the old black stove. I was starving by that time, and eagerly accepted.

We sat down to what old Mr. McNight called "a full English breakfast," of sausage, bacon, eggs, toast, and even a grilled tomato on the side. It was like old times. He made a pot of tea and listened gravely as I told him how that last year, 1946, had been the turning point in my life, after Daddy lost the job in Ruth with the Nevada Northern, in the same way he had lost the job here in Shafter with the Western Pacific. And about finding a happy, stable home with relatives who took me in and were now sending me to college.

It hadn't been easy. I had no idea what to expect upon arrival in that foreign state of Iowa, to begin a new life with strangers—lacking even a decent winter coat to keep me from freezing on a cold February morning.

My first impression of my Uncle Karl was that he was indeed a force to be reckoned with, as my gloomy old grandmother had warned. Stiff, unsmiling, and every inch a distinguished gentleman, I recalled her instruction to "watch your p's and q's" around the man! Naturally, I was terrified of him at first, but Aunt Rachel's warmth soon melted the ice.

If they were dismayed by the bedraggled waif standing before them in the same little seersucker suit that I had worn on the train to Shafter in 1945, they did their best to hide it. My mother's advice that summer ("it won't show the wrinkles") didn't hold up after three days on an over-heated Greyhound bus in the winter.

Later, while picking with some dismay through the few clothes in my little cardboard suitcase, Aunt Rachel came to a decision. No doubt realizing that I would be compared to—and criticized by—my classmates at the elite University of Iowa prep school where they had enrolled me, the first order of business was a new wardrobe. "Uncle Karl likes his women to look nice," she said firmly.

An hour later, with Aunt Rachel at the wheel, we were skidding into an icy parking place in front of a downtown department store, where I was to learn that Uncle Karl spared no expense in making "his women" look nice. For one whose clothes had always been made by my mother— sometimes cut down and made over from someone else's, and other times put together from leftover scraps of mate- rial—this was a unique experience.

After an exhausting day of shopping for everything from a warm winter coat to shoes and underwear, I carried all the bags and boxes up to the room I had been given and spread the contents out on the satin bedspread. I was being Shirley Temple again, in that little princess movie, after Cesar Romero had showered me with luxurious gifts! There was even a party dress, though it would be some time before anyone invited me to a party—or anything else, for that matter.

Meredith Wilson had it exactly right, in his *Music Man,* depicting Iowans as "by-God-stubborn" and standoffish. The new school (my third in that year of the eighth grade) might as well have had a NO ADMITTANCE sign above the door. On my first day in school I was introduced to each class by a girl who had been given that job by the principal. And I could tell she was wishing that he had picked on someone else! At lunch in the cafeteria that day, and every day, no one spoke to me. When they looked at me it was as if they saw an alien from another planet, with a tan and a ready smile. (You weren't supposed to have either one in Iowa.) From conversations at other tables, I gathered they thought California was another name for Hollywood, where they made movies. And the West, in general, was populated by cowboys and Indians, still shooting it out.

But having no social life at least gave me time to study and catch up to my class, scholastically. Due to inferior Nevada schools, I was almost a year behind in everything except English where, thanks to old Mr. McNight, my mastery of Shakespeare and classical literature again dazzled students and faculty alike.

After several weeks of the "silent treatment" from my peers, and having them look right through me in the halls, I decided on a drastic course of action.

If these bumpkins thought we did nothing but sing and dance and make movies out where I came from, I would give them something for lunch besides their meatloaf and mashed potatoes!

Walking through the cafeteria line, I filled my tray with the "props" I needed and carried it to an empty table. Then I went into my routine—Marjorie Main's song from the movie, *The Harvey Girls,* which I had just seen, and belting out (with gestures):

"Yer lookin' just as purty as a Spanish om-e-lette, but now I gotta teach ya how to get the table set!" Taking each object off my tray, as I sang, "First comes the plate, and then the cup and sass-y! Knife and fork, and here's yer spoon, and napkin by the glass-y!"

At the end of my number I circled the table with a few tap steps, and then sat down and calmly began eating my lunch. At first there was complete silence from gaping mouths all over the room, then a few titters broke out, and then full-scale laughter. There was even a round of hesitant applause, and finally a few shouts of "Hey, do that again!" (So of course I did.) A week later I had a date with a boy for a movie. The next month I wore my party dress twice.

There was not much more to tell about those happy years spent in Iowa, where I became a typical teenager, graduating high school with a decent, though not impressive, grade point average. "Seems to be majoring in boys," Uncle Karl would tell anyone who asked what I was studying the next year at the university.

Pouring us more tea, old Mr. McNight asked, "And your Lady Mother?"

Everyone in Shafter had seen my "Lady Mother" decamp to Salt Lake City with Sir Lancelot as soon as King Arthur's back was turned, so there was no need for deception.

"She's well," I said. "And unhappily married. Again."

"To Archibald Denney?"

"No. To another man, who turned out to be a bigger liar than Mr. Denney."

"Oh, what a tangled web we weave, when first we practice to deceive."

"Yes, and I hope Mr. Denney strangled in his! He talked my mother into going with him to Salt Lake City, presumably to wait for his wife to die. But it turned out that Mrs. Denney wasn't as far gone as he made out. For all I know, she's still alive." And I added, "Poor soul."

"Do you see them? Your mother and father?"

"I've seen her, and I intend to see Daddy on this trip. He lives in San Francisco with his new wife. I think he's happy, though I know he's never stopped loving my mother, as crazy as it sounds."

"I always liked your father. And your mother, too."

"I don't blame either of them for what they did. And I feel sorry for my mother. I know she regretted losing track of me that way. But she had no idea how things would turn out, and I can't condemn her for following her heart. She simply was not a very good judge of character. Especially in men. It's a shame, too, because she's been looking for true love all her life, and failed to recognize it when it was sitting right across the table from her. Some women are like that, I guess."

Old Mr. McNight looked sad, for the first time that morning. Was he thinking of Orvy's mother, Abby?

For no other reason than wanting to change the subject, I said, "What about your son and daughter-in-law, Mr. McNight? Are they still here in Shafter?"

"Oh, no. Orval and I were both laid off when the W.P. began phasing out steam engines and replacing them with diesels. He and Jean live in Wendover where he has a job with the Water Department."

(*Of course. Orvy, being an old water tower operator, would know something about water, wouldn't he?*) "Do you see them?"

"Not really. Orval is . . . very much like his mother, you know."

I certainly knew the big oaf wasn't anything like his father! "Who else is still here, then? Joe Thomas? Mrs. Hoppe?"

"Joe is around, usually on weekends. Grace moved to Elko with the children so they could go to high school. Mrs. Hoppe isn't qualified to teach high school."

She isn't qualified to teach elementary school, either, but we won't go into that. "And what's happened to the school, then?"

"Mrs. Hoppe still teaches there, but most of her students now are the children of the section men, and that little Hernandez girl is a great help to her."

So, little Nita, who would be in the sixth grade now, had become a "student-teacher" just the way I had! I was pleased about that.

"I saw that the depot was closed and the sign said 'No

trains.' What does that mean? Don't they have an agent here anymore?"

"No. Diesel engines have killed Shafter, whose lifeblood was coal and water during the age of steam. I expect everyone will be gone one day."

"And what about you, Mr. McNight? Will you be going, too?"

"What, and leave all my friends?" He swept an arm around the cozy, untidy room, where books were still stacked everywhere on shelves and tables.

It was a shame about the Western Pacific, he said. There were those who called it "the railroad that was built too late," and "The Wobbly," whose initials mostly stood for "Willing People." It was, in fact, a "bridge" railroad, dependent on separate carriers at either end for its support. Even Mother Nature had turned against the W.P., sending storms that buried tracks and trains under mountain avalanches. It was plagued with receiverships and attempted hostile takeovers and strikes. There had been a major strike, just last year, that had created "a streak of rust across the desert," according to a rival railroad executive. Nothing moved for months. Management blamed Labor and Labor, in turn, blamed Management, but there was plenty of blame to go around. He predicted that the "Little Railroad That Could," which had been like family to all of us, could not endure much more. Even the popular Exposition Flyer had been in so many accidents, due to poor track maintenance, that it was derisively being called the "*Explosion* Flyer!" It was sad to think of my beloved "Flyer" that way.

I looked at my watch. We had been talking for over two hours! I knew I should be going, but I wanted to say something before I left. At the door I turned back and said, "You know, Mr. McNight, I learned more from you, right here in this room, than I ever did in any classroom, including my college courses! Thank you."

The old man blinked his eyes several times and seemed unable to speak.

It was getting late, but there was one other thing I wanted to do.

"I think I'll just walk down by the corral before I go."

"She's not there now. I don't expect her back much before the snow flies."

"Who?"

"Your white horse."

Then he explained that Dusty had reappeared the next year after I left. It had been an usually severe winter, the ground had been covered in snow for months, and animals were suffering from lack of food. He had found her one day, inside the corral, trying to get a drink from the frozen water trough. She was so thin her ribs showed beneath her shaggy coat. She was obviously looking for me, he said, but didn't run away when she saw him, so he opened the shed where I had left hay and oats, and gave her a good deal of it. She was still there the next day and the day after that, so he kept on feeding her—he and Joe Thomas—until the snow melted. And then, one day she was gone.

Dusty! My beautiful horse, so fat and sleek when I left! To think of her now—thin and hungry! But what did he mean, he "didn't expect her back before the snow flies?"

"Oh, she comes back every year, now. To spend the winter with us."

"And you continue to feed her? You and Joe Thomas?"

"Yes."

I suspected that old Mr. McNight was living on a small Western Pacific pension. I reached into my purse and took out the crisp new hundred-dollar bill that Uncle Karl had put there, and tucked it inside a book of poetry on the table.

"I'd like to contribute to Dusty's support," I said. When he started to protest, I added, "A very kind and generous man gave me that money. I'm only passing it on to another one."

He understood. He nodded and thanked me.

I had one more question for him. "Do you think that Dusty felt, you know . . . abandoned . . . when I left her?"

"Did you? Did you feel abandoned?"

"Yes."

"But you didn't blame your parents. I'm sure she didn't blame you, either."

"I was lucky. But it breaks my heart to think of my poor horse being *hungry!*"

"Oh, she had another reason for coming back. She wanted to show you something!"

"What was it?"

"A beautiful white colt."

Now I was crying for joy! She'd found other wild mustangs that accepted her. Old Mr. McNight went on to explain that he and Joe had been afraid the mare and her colt might be picked up by the mustang trader. So they watched for him, and the next time he showed up, Joe told him that he had bought the two horses from me. They were easily recognized, being a distinctive color, and if he should ever see them again, the man was to understand that they belonged to him, and leave them alone.

So now she was free to roam and mingle with her own kind, but to come back here to the people who had befriended her, whenever she wanted to! I was so grateful that I completely forgot myself and threw my arms around the astonished old man!

I did walk out to the corral after we'd said goodbye, but with a light heart. I climbed up on the top rail of the corral and thought about Dusty. She *had* felt abandoned. I *knew* she had. But she'd been lucky, too. We had *both* found good people who protected and cared for us.

It was another long day's drive to my first destination in California, my sister's and brother-in-law's house in the San Francisco Bay Area, where I would rest for a day or two before delivering the car to its new owner in San Jose. I had seen my sister only once since that short visit to Shafter in 1945. Three years later, when I was a sophomore in high school, she came to Iowa to see me. After that we had kept in touch and become quite close.

Recently, there had been an invitation to spend the summer with her and Rudy Vallee (I would always think of him that way). They were still a childless couple, and I suspected that my sister was lonely. So I had decided to accept her invitation, but with every intention of returning to Iowa in time to register as a sophomore at the university.

Ah, the best laid plans of mice and men! My own plans were derailed that summer by falling in love. And whether

My sister and I in Iowa, 1948

you called what was going on in Korea a "police action" or a war, it amounted to the same thing. Like my sister in the previous war, I fell for a uniform.

But that's another story.